The Princess and the Goblin

The Princess and the Goblin

by George MacDonald

Chariot Books
DAVID C. COOK PUBLISHING CO.

Illustrated by Linda Hill Griffith

For my parents,
Bill and Yvonne Hill
—L. H. G.

Chariot Books is an imprint of David C. Cook Publishing Co.
David C. Cook Publishing Co., Elgin, IL 60120
David C. Cook Publishing Co., Weston, Ontario

THE PRINCESS AND THE GOBLIN
Edited text © 1985 by David C. Cook Publishing Co.
Illustrations © 1985 by Linda Hill Griffith

First printing, 1985

Printed in the United States of America
90 89 88 87 86 85   5 4 3 2 1

Library of Congress Cataloging in Publication Data

MacDonald, George, 1824-1905.
   The princess and the goblin.

   (Chariot classics)
   Summary: A little princess is protected by her friend Curdie from the goblin miners who live beneath the castle.
   [1. Fairy tales] I. Griffith, Linda Hill, ill.
II. Title.
PZ7.M1754Pr   1983   [Fic]   82-1421
ISBN 0-89191-557-5

CONTENTS

1   The Princess Loses Herself   7

2   What the Nurse Thought of It   14

3   The Little Miner   18

4   The Goblins   27

5   The Hall of the Goblin Palace   35

6   The Old Lady's Room   42

7   The Cobs' Creatures   51

8   The Very Next Week   55

9   The Ring   64

10   Goblin Counsels   67

11   Irene's Thread   77

12   The Old Lady and Curdie   89

13   Curdie and His Mother   95

14   Curdie Comes to Grief   101

15   Goblins in the King's House   108

16   The Underground Waters   118

1   The Princess Loses Herself

There was once a little princess whose father was king over a great country full of mountains and valleys. His grand and beautiful palace was built upon one of the mountains. The princess, whose name was Irene, was born there. But because her mother was not very strong, Irene was sent away to live with country people in a large house on the side of another mountain, about halfway between its base and its peak.

The princess was a sweet little creature of eight when our story begins. Her face was fair and pretty, with eyes like two bits of night sky, each with a star dissolved in the blue. The ceiling of her nursery was blue also, with stars in it, as like the sky as they could make it. But I doubt if ever she saw the real night sky, for her guardians were too afraid of a strange race of beings, called by some gnomes, by some kobolds, by some goblins.

These creatures lived in hollow places underneath the mountains—huge caverns, and winding ways, some with water running through them, and some shining with all colors of the rainbow when a light was taken in. There would not have been much known about them, had there not been mines there, which had been dug to get at the ore of which the mountains were full.

There was a legend that at one time the goblins had lived above ground, and

7

were very like other people. But for some reason or other, the king had laid what they thought were too severe taxes upon them, or had required observances of them they did not like, or had begun to impose stricter laws. And the consequence was that they had all disappeared from the face of the country.

Instead of going to some other country, they had all taken refuge in the caverns. They never came out except at night, and then seldom showed themselves in any numbers—and never to many people at once. Those who had caught sight of them said that they had greatly altered in the course of generations; and no wonder, seeing they lived away from the sun, in cold and wet and dark places. They were now, not ordinarily ugly—but absolutely hideous, both in face and form.

As the goblins grew misshapen in body they had grown in knowledge and cleverness. Now they were able to do things no mortal could see the possibility of. But as they grew in cunning, they grew in mischief. Their great delight was to annoy the people who lived in the open-air above them in every way they could think of. They so heartily cherished the ancient grudge against those who occupied their former possessions, and especially against the descendants of the king, that they sought every opportunity to torment them. In the process of time they had gotten a king and a government of their own, whose chief business, beyond their own simple affairs, was to devise trouble for their neighbors.

One very wet day, when the mountain was covered with mist that was constantly gathering itself together into raindrops, and pouring down on the roofs of the great old house, the princess could not of course go out-of-doors. She got very tired, so tired that even her toys could no longer amuse her.

The princess was sitting in the nursery with the sky ceiling over her head, leaning with her back bowed into the back of the chair, her head hanging down, and her hands in her lap, very miserable, not even knowing what she would like to do, except to go out and get thoroughly wet, and catch a particularly nasty cold, and have to go to bed and eat gruel.

The next moment her nurse went out of the room. Even that seemed to be a change in such a dreary day, so the princess woke up a little, and looked about her. Then she tumbled off her chair, and ran out of the door, not the same door the nurse went out of, but one which opened at the foot of a curious old stair of worm-eaten oak, which looked as if no one had ever set foot upon it. She had once before been up six steps of the staircase, which was sufficient reason on such a day for trying to find out what was at the top of it.

Up and up she ran—such a long way it seemed to her!—until she came to the top of the third flight. There she found the end of a long passage, which was full of doors on each side. There were so many that she did not care to open any, but ran through the corridor and on to the end, where she turned into another passage, also full of doors. When she had turned twice more, and still saw doors—and only doors—about her, she began to get frightened.

It was so silent! And all those doors must hide rooms with nobody in them! The princess turned and started at full speed back for the stairs and her safe nursery, her little footsteps echoing through the sounds of the rain, which made a trampling noise on the roof.

She ran for some distance, turned several times, and then began to be afraid. Very soon she was sure she had lost the way back. But she was too eager and perhaps too frightened to cry for some time. At last her hope failed her. Nothing but passages and doors everywhere! She threw herself on the floor, and burst into sobs.

She did not cry long, however, for she was as brave as could be expected of a princess of her age. After a good cry, she got up, and brushed the dust from her frock. Then she wiped her eyes with her hands, for princesses don't always have their handkerchiefs in their pockets, any more than some other little girls.

Next, like a true princess, she resolved to try again to find her way back: she would walk through the passages, and look in every direction for the stair. This she did, but without success. She went over the same ground again and again without knowing it, for the passages and doors were all alike. At last, in a corner, through a half-open door, she did see a stair. But, alas! It went the wrong way: instead of going down, it went up.

She could not help wishing to see where the stair led. It was narrow, and so steep that she went up like a four-legged creature on her hands and feet.

When she came to the top, she found herself in a little square place, with three doors, two opposite each other, and one opposite the top of the stair. She stood for a moment, without an idea in her little head what to do next. But as she stood, she began to hear a curious humming sound. It was much more gentle, and even more monotonous than the sound of the rain, which she scarcely heard now.

Where could the humming come from? She laid her ear first to one of the doors, then to another. When she laid her ear against the third door, there could be no doubt that the sound came from something in that room. She was rather afraid, but her curiosity was stronger than her fear, and she opened the door very gently and peeped in. What do you think she saw? A very old lady at a spinning wheel.

Perhaps you will wonder how the princess could tell that she was an old lady, when I inform you that not only was she beautiful, but her skin was smooth and white. Her hair was combed back from her forehead and face, and hung loose far down her back. That is not much like an old lady, is it? Ah! but her hair was white almost as snow. And although her face was so smooth, her eyes looked so wise that you could not have helped seeing she must be old.

The princess, though she could not have told you why, did think her very old indeed. *Quite fifty*, she said to herself.

While the princess stared bewildered, with her head just inside the door, the old lady lifted hers, and said, in a sweet, but old and rather shaky voice, "Come in, my dear; come in. I am glad to see you."

The princess stepped inside the door at once, and shut it gently behind her. She approached the old lady rather slowly until she stood by her side, and looked up in her face with her blue eyes and the two melted stars in them.

"Why, what have you been doing with your eyes, child?" asked the old lady.

"Crying, because I couldn't find my way down again."

"But your face is streaked like the back of a zebra. Why didn't you come to me to wipe your eyes for you?"

"Please, I didn't know you were here. I will next time."

"There's a good child!" The old lady stopped her wheel, and rose, and, going out of the room, returned with a little silver basin and a soft white towel, with which she washed and wiped the bright little face.

When she carried away the basin and towel, the little princess wondered to see how straight and tall the lady was, for, although she was so old, she didn't stoop a bit. She was dressed in black velvet with thick, white, heavy-looking lace about it; and on the black dress her hair shone like silver. There was hardly any more furniture in the room than there might have been in the cottage of the poorest old woman who made her bread by her spinning. There was no carpet on the floor—no table anywhere—nothing but the spinning wheel and the chair beside it.

When the beautiful lady came back, she sat down again, and without a word began her spinning once more, while Irene, who had never seen a spinning wheel, stood by her side and looked on. When the old lady had her thread going again, she said to the princess, without looking at her: "Do you know my name, child?"

"No, I don't know it," answered the princess.

"My name is Irene."

"That's *my* name!"

"I know that; I let you have mine. I haven't got your name. You've got mine."

"How can that be?" asked the princess, bewildered. "I've always had my name."

"Your papa, the king, asked me if I had any objection to your having it; and, of course, I hadn't. I let you have it with pleasure. A name is one of those things one can give away and keep all the same. I have a good many such things. Wouldn't you like to know who I am, child?"

"Yes, that I should—very much."

"I'm your great-great-grandmother."

"What's that?" asked the princess.

"I'm your father's mother's father's mother."

"Oh, dear! I can't understand that."

"I daresay not. I didn't expect you would. I will explain it all to you when you are older," the lady went on. "But you will be able to understand this much now: I came here to take care of you."

"Is it long since you came? Was it yesterday?"

"I've been here ever since you came yourself."

"What a long time!" said the princess. "But I never saw you before. Do you live in this room always?"

"I don't sleep in it. I sleep on the opposite side of the landing. I sit here most of the day."

"I shouldn't like it here. My nursery is much prettier. But you must be a queen, too, if you are my great big grandmother."

"Yes, I am a queen."

"I wonder why nursie never told me."

"Nursie doesn't know. She never saw me. Nobody knows I am in the house."

"How do you get your dinner, then?" asked Irene.

"I keep poultry—of a sort."

"And who makes the chicken broth for you?"

"I never kill any of my chickens."

"Then I can't understand."

"What did you have for breakfast this morning?" asked the lady.

"Oh! I had bread and milk, and an egg—I daresay you eat their eggs. Is that what makes your hair so white?"

"No, my dear. It's old age. I am very old."

"I thought so. Are you fifty?"

"Yes—more than that."

"Are you a hundred?"

"Yes—more than that. I am too old for you to guess. Come and see my chickens."

She rose, took the princess by the hand, led her out of the room, and opened the door opposite the stair. The princess expected to see a lot of hens and chickens, but instead of that, she saw the blue sky first, and then the roofs of the house, with a multitude of the loveliest pigeons, mostly white, but of all colors, walking about, making bows to each other, and talking a language she could not understand.

"What very nice poultry! Are the eggs nice?"

"Yes, very nice."

"But how do you get at the eggs? Where are their nests?"

The lady took hold of a little loop of string in the wall at the side of the door and, lifting a shutter, showed a great many pigeonholes with nests, some with young pigeons and some with eggs in them. She closed it again quickly, lest the young ones should be frightened.

"Oh, what a nice way!" cried the princess. "Will you give me an egg to eat? I'm rather hungry."

"I will someday, but now you must go back. I daresay nursie's looking for you everywhere."

"Except here," answered the princess. "Oh, how surprised she will be when I tell her about my great big grand-grandmother!"

"Yes, that she will!" said the old lady with a curious smile. "Mind you tell her all about it exactly. I will take you to the top of the stair, and then you must run down quite fast into your own room."

The little princess put her hand in the old lady's, who, looking this way and that, brought her to the top of the first stairway, and thence to the bottom of the second, and did not leave her till she saw her halfway down the third. When she heard the cry of her nurse's pleasure at finding her, she turned and walked up the stairs again, very fast indeed for such a very great grandmother.

2   What the Nurse Thought of It

"Why, where can you have been, princess?" asked the nurse, taking Irene in her arms. "It's very unkind of you to hide away so long. I began to be afraid—"

Here she checked herself.

"What were you afraid of, nursie?" asked the princess.

"Never mind," she answered. "Perhaps I will tell you another day. Now tell me where you have been."

"I've been up a long way to see my very great, huge, old grandmother."

"What do you mean by that?" asked the nurse, who thought she was making fun.

"I mean that I've been a long way up and up to see my great-grandmother. Ah, nursie, you don't know what a beautiful mother of grandmothers I've got upstairs. She is such an old lady! with such lovely white hair—as white as my silver cup. Now, when I think of it, I think her hair must be silver."

"What nonsense you are talking, princess!"

"I'm not talking nonsense," returned Irene, rather offended. "I will tell you all about her. She's much taller than you, and much prettier."

"Oh, I daresay!" remarked the nurse.

"And she lives upon pigeons' eggs."

"Most likely," said the nurse.

"And she sits in an empty room, spin-spinning all day long."

"Not a doubt of it," said the nurse.

"And she's been there ever since I came here—ever so many years."

"Anybody could have told you that," said the nurse, who did not believe a word Irene was saying.

"You don't believe me, then!" exclaimed the princess, astonished and angry, as she well might be.

"Did you expect me to believe you, princess?" asked the nurse coldly. "I know princesses are in the habit of telling make-believes. But you are the first I ever heard of who expected to have them believed," she added, seeing that the child was strangely in earnest.

The princess burst into tears. "But it's quite true, I tell you."

"You've dreamt it, then, child."

"No, I didn't dream it. I went upstairs, and I lost myself, and if I hadn't found the beautiful lady, I should never have found myself. Just come up with me, and see if I'm not telling the truth."

"Indeed I have other work to do. It's your dinnertime, and I won't have any more such nonsense."

The princess wiped her eyes, and her face grew so hot that her tears were soon quite dry. She sat down to her dinner, but ate next to nothing. Not to be believed does not at all agree with princesses, for a real princess cannot tell a lie. So all the afternoon she did not speak a word.

Of course the nurse was not comfortable in her mind. She loved the princess dearly, and was vexed with herself for having been cross to her. As it became more and more plain by Irene's every motion and look during the evening that her heart was too vexed and troubled to enjoy her toys, her nurse's discomfort grew and grew. When bedtime came, the child, instead of holding up her little mouth to be kissed, turned away from her and lay still.

Then nursie's heart gave way altogether, and she began to cry. At the sound of her first sob the princess turned again, and held her face to kiss her as usual. But the nurse had her handkerchief to her eyes and did not see the movement.

"Nursie," said the princess, "why won't you believe me?"

"Because I *can't* believe you," said the nurse, getting angry again.

"Ah! Then you can't help it, Lootie"—that was Irene's pet name for her nurse—"and I will not be vexed with you anymore. I will give you a kiss and go to sleep."

"You little angel!" cried the nurse, and caught her out of bed, and walked about the room with her in her arms, kissing and hugging her.

15

"You will let me take you to see my dear old great big grandmother, won't you?" said the princess, as she laid her down again.

"And you won't say I'm ugly, anymore—will you, princess?"

"Nursie, I never said you were ugly. What can you mean?"

"You said I wasn't so pretty as that—"

"As my beautiful grandmother—yes, I did say that, for it's quite true."

"Then I do think you are unkind!" said the nurse, and put her handkerchief to her eyes again.

"Nursie, dear, you are very nice-looking, but if you had been as beautiful as my grandmother some king or other would have married you, and then what would have become of me?"

"You are an angel!" said the nurse, again embracing her.

"Now," insisted Irene, "you will come and see my grandmother—won't you?"

"I will go with you anywhere you like, my cherub," she answered. And in two minutes the weary little princess was fast asleep.

When the princess woke the next morning, she heard the rain still falling. Indeed, this day was so like the last that it would have been difficult to tell what was the use of it. The first thing she thought of was the lady in the tower; and the first question that occupied her thoughts was whether she should ask the nurse to fulfill her promise this very morning.

But she came to the conclusion that perhaps the lady would not be pleased if she took anyone to see her without first asking, especially as it was pretty evident—seeing she lived on pigeons' eggs and cooked them herself—that she did not want the household to know she was there. So the princess resolved to take the first opportunity to run up alone and ask if she might bring her nurse.

The princess and her nurse were the best of friends all during dressing time, and the princess in consequence ate an enormous little breakfast before she went to play.

Now the nurse could not be every moment in the room, and because before yesterday the princess had never given her the smallest reason for anxiety, it had not yet come into Lootie's head to watch her more closely. So the nurse soon gave her a chance to escape, and Irene was off and up the stairs again.

This day's adventure, however, did not turn out like yesterday's. The princess ran through passage after passage, and could not find the stair of the tower. When she turned to go back, she failed equally in her search after the stair. She was lost once more.

It was no wonder that she cried again. Suddenly it occurred to her that it was after having cried before that she had found her grandmother's stair. She got up at once, wiped her eyes, and started upon a fresh quest. This time, although she did not come on a stair that went up, she came upon one that went down. So down she went, and, to her surprise, she found herself in the kitchen. Although she was not allowed to go there alone, her nurse had often taken her, and she was a great favorite with the servants. So there was a general rush at her the moment she appeared, for everyone wanted to have her; and the report of where she was soon reached the nurse's ears. She came at once to fetch her; but she never suspected how the princess had gotten there.

Irene's failure to find the old lady not only disappointed her, but made her very thoughtful. Sometimes she came almost to the nurse's opinion that she had dreamed all about her. She wondered much whether she should ever see her again, and thought it very sad not to have been able to find her. She resolved to say nothing more to her nurse on the subject, seeing it was so little in her power to prove her words.

3   The Little Miner

The next day the great cloud still hung over the mountain, and the rain poured like water from a full sponge. The princess was very fond of being out-of-doors, and she nearly cried when she saw that the weather was no better. But the mist was not of such a dark, dingy gray; there was light in it. And as the hours went on, it grew brighter and brighter, until it was almost too brilliant to look at. Late in the afternoon the sun broke out so gloriously that Irene clapped her hands, crying: "See, see, Lootie! The sun has had his face washed. Look how bright he is! Do get my hat, and let us go out for a walk."

Lootie was very glad to please the princess. She got her hat and cloak, and they set out together for a walk up the mountain. The clouds were rolling away in broken pieces, like great, over woolly sheep. Between them the sky shone with a deeper and purer blue because of the rain. The trees on the roadside were hung all over with drops, which sparkled in the sun like jewels. Irene was in raptures, and Lootie shared in her delight, for she, too, had been confined to the house for three days.

At length Lootie observed that the sun was getting low, and said it was time to be going back. She made the remark again and again. But every time the princess begged her to go on just a little farther and a little farther, reminding her that it was much easier to go downhill, and saying that when they did turn

18

they would be at home in a moment. So on and on they went, now to look at a group of ferns over whose tops a stream was pouring in a watery arch, now to pick a shining stone from a rock by the wayside, now to watch the flight of some bird.

Suddenly the shadow of a great mountain peak came up from behind, and shot in front of them. When the nurse saw it, she started and shook, and catching hold of the princess's hand turned and began to run down the hill.

"What's all the haste, nursie?" asked Irene, running alongside of her.

"We must not be out a moment longer."

"But we can't help being out a good many moments longer."

It was too true. They were much too far from home. It was against express orders to be out with the princess one moment after the sun was down, and they were nearly a mile up the mountain! If His Majesty, Irene's papa, were to hear of it, Lootie would certainly be dismissed; and to leave the princess would break her heart. It was no wonder she ran. But Irene was not in the least frightened, not knowing anything to be frightened at.

"Lootie! Lootie! why do you run so fast? It shakes my teeth when I talk."

"Then don't talk," said Lootie.

But the princess went on talking. She was always saying: "Look, look, Lootie!" But Lootie paid no more heed to anything she said, only ran on.

"Look, look, Lootie! Don't you see that funny man peeping over the rock?"

Lootie only ran the faster. They had to pass the rock, and when they came nearer, the princess saw it was only a lump of the rock itself that she had taken for a man.

"Look, look, Lootie! There's such a curious creature at the foot of that old tree. Look at it, Lootie! It's making faces at us, I do think."

Lootie gave a stifled cry, and ran faster still—so fast that Irene's little legs could not keep up with her, and she fell with a crash. It was a hard, downhill road, and she had been running very fast, so it was no wonder she began to cry. This put the nurse nearly beside herself, but all she could do was to run on the moment she got the princess on her feet again.

"Who's that laughing at me?" asked the princess, trying to keep in her sobs, and running too fast for her grazed knees.

"Nobody, child," said the nurse, almost angrily.

But that instant there came a burst of coarse tittering from somewhere near, and a hoarse, indistinct voice that seemed to say: "Lies! Lies! Lies!"

"Oh!" cried the nurse with a sound that was almost a scream, and ran on faster than ever.

"Nursie! Lootie! I can't run anymore. Do let us walk a bit."

"What *am* I to do?" said the nurse. "Here, I will carry you."

She caught her up, but found her much too heavy to run with and had to set her down again. Then she looked wildly about her, gave a great cry, and said: "We've taken the wrong turn somewhere, and I don't know where we are. We are lost!"

The terror she was in had quite bewildered her. It was true enough they had lost the way. They had been running down into a little valley in which there was no house to be seen.

Now Irene did not know what good reason there was for her nurse's terror, for the servants all had strict orders never to mention the goblins to her. But it was very distressing to see her nurse in such a fright. Before she had time to grow thoroughly alarmed, Irene heard the sound of whistling. Presently she saw a boy coming up the road from the valley to meet them. He was the whistler; but before they met his whistling changed to singing.

> "Ring! dod! bang!
> Go the hammers' clang!
> Hit and turn and bore!
> Whizz and puff and roar!
> Thus we rive the rocks,
> Force the goblin locks.
> See the shining ore!
> One, two, three—
> Bright as gold can be!
> Four, five, six—
> Shovels, mattocks, picks!
>
> Seven, eight, nine—
> Light your lamp at mine.
> Ten, eleven, twelve—
> Loosely hold the helve.
> We're the merry miner boys,
> Make the goblins hold their noise."

"I wish you would hold your noise," said the nurse rudely, for the very word *goblin* at such a time and in such a place made her tremble. It would bring the goblins upon them for a certainty to defy them in that way. But whether the boy heard her or not, he did not stop singing.

"Hush! scush! scurry!
There you go in a hurry!
Gobble! gobble! goblin!
There you go a wobblin';
Hobble, hobble, hobblin'!
Cobble! cobble! cobblin'!
Hob-bob-goblin!—Huuuuuh!"

"There!" said the boy, as he stood still opposite them. "There! that'll do for them. They can't bear singing, and they can't stand that song. They can't sing themselves, for they have no more voice than a crow. And they don't like other people to sing."

The boy was dressed in a miner's dress, with a curious cap on his head. He was a very nice-looking boy of twelve, with eyes as dark as the mines in which he worked and as sparkling as the crystals in their rocks. His face was almost too pale, which came from his being so little in the open air and the sunlight, for even vegetables grown in the dark are white. But he looked happy, merry indeed—perhaps at the thought of having routed the goblins. His bearing as he stood before them had nothing clownish or rude about it.

"I saw them," he went on, "as I came up; and I'm very glad I did. I knew they were after somebody, but I couldn't see who it was. They won't touch you so long as I'm with you."

"Why, who are you?" asked the nurse, offended at the freedom with which he spoke to them.

"I'm Peter's son."

"Who's Peter?"

"Peter the miner."

"And why should the goblins mind you, pray?"

"Because I don't mind them. I'm used to them."

"What difference does that make?"

"If you're not afraid of them, they're afraid of you. I'm not afraid of them. That's all. But it's all that's wanted—up here, that is. It's a different thing down in the mine. They won't always mind that song down there. If anyone sings it, they stand grinning at him awfully. And if he gets frightened, and misses a word, or says a wrong one—oh! don't they give it to him!"

"What do they do to him?" asked Irene, with a trembling voice.

"Don't go frightening the princess," warned the nurse.

"The princess!" repeated the little miner, taking off his curious cap. "I beg

21

your pardon, but you oughtn't to be out so late. Everybody knows that's against the law.''

"Yes, indeed it is!'' said the nurse, beginning to cry again. "And I shall have to suffer for it.''

"I hope they didn't hear you call her the princess,'' said the boy. "If they did, they're sure to know her again; they're awfully sharp.''

"Lootie! Lootie!'' cried the princess. "Take me home.''

"Don't go on like that,'' said the nurse to the boy, almost fiercely. "How could I help it? I lost my way.''

"You wouldn't have lost your way if you hadn't been frightened,'' said the boy. "Come along. I'll soon set you right again. Shall I carry Your Highness?''

"No, thank you,'' said Irene. "I can walk very well, though I can't run so fast as nursie. If you will give me one hand, Lootie will give me another, and then I shall get on famously.''

They soon had her between them, holding a hand of each.

"Now let's run,'' said the nurse.

"No, no,'' said the little miner. "That's the worst thing you can do. If you hadn't run before, you would not have lost your way. And if you run now, they will be after you in a moment.''

So they went on, walking pretty fast, but taking care not to run a step.

"I want to talk to you,'' Irene said to the little miner. "But it's so awkward! I don't know your name.''

"My name's Curdie, little princess.''

"What a funny name! Curdie! What more?''

"Curdie Peterson. What's your name, please?''

"Irene.''

"What more?''

"I don't know what more. What more is my name, Lootie?''

"Princesses haven't got more than one name. They don't want it.''

"Oh, then, Curdie, you must call me just Irene and no more.''

"No, indeed,'' said the nurse indignantly. "He shall say, 'Your Royal Highness.' ''

"My Royal Highness! What's that? No, no, Lootie, I won't be called names. I don't like them. Curdie, my name's Irene.''

"Well, Irene,'' said Curdie, with a glance at the nurse, which showed he enjoyed teasing her, "it is very kind of you to let me call you anything. I like your name very much.''

He expected the nurse to interfere again, but he soon saw that she was too frightened to speak. She was staring at something a few yards before them in the middle of the path, where it narrowed between rocks so that only one could pass at a time.

"It is very kind of you to go out of your way to take us home," said Irene.

"I'm not going out of my way yet," said Curdie. "The path turns off to my father's on the other side of those rocks."

"You wouldn't think of leaving us till we're safe home, I'm sure," gasped the nurse.

"Of course not," said Curdie.

"You dear, good, kind Curdie! I'll give you a kiss when we get home," said the princess.

The nurse gave her a great pull by the hand she held. But at that instant that something in the middle of the way, which had looked like a great lump of earth, began to move. One after another it shot out four long things, like two arms and two legs. The nurse began to tremble from head to foot. Irene clasped Curdie's hand yet harder, and Curdie began to sing again:

> "One, two—
> Hit and hew!
> Three, four—
> Blast and bore!
> Five, six—
> There's a fix!
> Seven, eight—
> Hold it straight!
> Nine, ten—
> Hit again!
> Hurry! scurry!
> Bother! smother!
> There's a toad
> In the road—
> Smash it! Squash it!
> Fry it! Dry it!
> You're another!
> Up and off!
> There's enough!—Huuuuuh!"

As he uttered the last words, Curdie let go his hold of his companion and rushed at the thing in the road as if he would trample it under his feet. It gave a great spring, and ran straight up one of the rocks like a huge spider. Curdie turned back laughing, and took Irene's hand again. She grasped his very tightly, but said nothing till they had passed the rocks. A few yards more and she found herself on a part of the road she knew, and was able to speak again.

"Do you know, Curdie, I don't quite like your song. It sounds rather rude to me," she said.

"Well, perhaps it is," answered Curdie. "I never thought of that; it's a way we have. We do it because they don't like it."

"Who don't like it?"

"The cobs, as we call them."

"Don't!" said the nurse.

"Why not?" said Curdie.

"I beg you don't. Please don't."

"Oh! if you ask me that way, of course, I won't; though I don't a bit know why. Look! There are the lights of your great house down below. You'll be at home in five minutes now."

They reached home in safety. Nobody had missed them, or even known they had gone out, and they arrived at the door belonging to their part of the house without anyone seeing them. The nurse was rushing in with a hurried and not overgracious good night to Curdie. But the princess pulled her hand from hers, and was just throwing her arms around Curdie's neck, when the nurse caught her again and dragged her away.

"Lootie! Lootie! I promised a kiss," cried Irene.

"A princess mustn't give kisses. It's not at all proper," said Lootie. "He's only a miner boy."

"He's a good boy, and a brave boy, and he has been very kind to us. Lootie! Lootie! I promised."

"Your Royal Highness," said Lootie, suddenly grown very respectful, "must come in directly."

"Nurse, a princess must not break her word," said Irene, drawing herself up and standing stock-still.

Lootie did not know which the king might count the worst: to let the princess be out after sunset or to let her kiss a miner boy. She did not know that, however much he might have disliked his daughter to kiss the miner boy, he would not have had her break her word for all the goblins in creation. But the nurse was not lady enough to understand this. Here Curdie again came to the rescue.

"Never mind, Princess Irene," he said. "You mustn't kiss me tonight. But you shan't break your word. I will come another time. You may be sure I will."

24

"Oh, thank you, Curdie!" said the princess, and stopped crying.

"Good night, Irene. Good night, Lootie," said Curdie, and turned and was out of sight in a moment.

"I should like to see him come back!" muttered the nurse, and said no more. She did not want to open a new cause of strife with the princess by saying more plainly what she meant. Glad enough that she had succeeded both in getting home unseen, and in keeping the princess from kissing the miner's boy, she resolved to watch her far better in future.

4 The Goblins

Curdie went home whistling. He resolved to say nothing about the princess for fear of getting the nurse into trouble, for while he enjoyed teasing her, he was careful not to do her any harm. He saw no more of the goblins, and was soon fast asleep in his bed.

He woke in the middle of the night, and thought he heard curious noises outside. He sat up and listened; then got up, and, opening the door very quietly, went out. When he peeped around the corner, he saw, under his own window, a group of stumpy creatures, whom he at once recognized by their shape. Hardly had he begun his "One, two, three . . ." when they broke asunder and were out of sight. He returned laughing, got into bed again, and was fast asleep in a moment.

Reflecting a little over the matter in the morning, he came to the conclusion that, as nothing of the kind had ever happened to him before, the goblins must be annoyed with him for protecting the princess. By the time he was dressed, however, he was thinking of something quite different, for he did not value the enmity of the goblins in the least.

As soon as they had had breakfast, he set off with his father for the mine. They entered the hill by a natural opening under a huge rock where a little stream rushed out. Curdie and his father followed its course for a few yards, and then the passage took a turn, and sloped steeply into the heart of the hill. With many angles and windings and branchings-off, it led them deep into the hill before they arrived at the place where they were digging out the precious ore. With flint and steel and tinderbox, they lighted their lamps, then fixed them on their heads, and were soon hard at work with their pickaxes and shovels and hammers.

Father and son were at work near each other, but not in the same gang (the passages out of which the ore was dug, they called gangs). For when the lode, or vein of ore, was small, one miner would have to dig away alone in a passage that just gave him room to work in uncomfortable, cramped positions. If the miners stopped for a moment, they could hear everywhere around them the sounds of their companions burrowing away in all directions in the inside of the great mountain. The work was hard at best, for it is very warm underground; but it was not particularly unpleasant.

When some of the miners wanted to earn a little more money for a particular purpose, they would work all night. You could not tell night from day down there, except for feeling tired and sleepy, because no light of the sun ever came into those gloomy regions. Some who had remained behind during the night would declare that they heard a tap-tapping all about them, as if the mountain were then more full of miners than ever it was during the day. And some would never stay overnight, for all knew those were the sounds of the goblins, who worked only at night. For the miners' night was the goblins' day.

Indeed, the greater number of the miners were afraid of the goblins. There were strange stories of the treatment some had received when the goblins had surprised them at their work during the night. But the more courageous of them, like Peter Peterson and Curdie, had stayed in the mine all night again and again. Although they had several times encountered a few stray goblins, they had never yet failed to drive them away.

The chief defense against them was verse, for they hated verse of every kind, and some kinds they could not endure at all. I suspect they could not make any rhymes themselves, and that was why they disliked it so much. Those miners who were never afraid were those who could make verses for themselves. For although there were certain old rhymes that were very effectual, yet it was well known that a new rhyme of the right sort was even more distasteful to the goblins, and therefore more effectual in putting them to flight.

Curdie had determined to remain in the mine alone this night if his father would permit him. He wanted to get extra wages to buy a red petticoat for his mother, and he had just a faint hope of finding out what the goblins were doing under his window the night before.

When he told his father, he made no objection, for he had great confidence in his boy's courage and resources.

"I'm sorry I can't stay with you," said Peter. "You'll be sure to take care of yourself, won't you?"

"Yes, father. I'll keep a sharp lookout, I promise you."

About six o'clock the rest of the miners went away, everyone bidding him good night and telling him to take care of himself; for he was a great favorite with them all.

"Don't forget your rhymes," said one.

"I'll do my best," said Curdie. "I'm not afraid."

"We all know that," they returned, and left him.

For some time Curdie worked away briskly, throwing all the ore he had disengaged on one side behind him to carry out in the morning. He heard a good deal of goblin tapping, but it all sounded far away in the hill, and he paid it little heed. Towards midnight he began to feel rather hungry. He dropped his pickax, got out a lump of bread, which in the morning he had laid in a damp hole in the rock, sat down on a heap of ore, and ate his supper. Then he leaned his head against the rock for five minutes' rest before beginning his work again.

He had not kept the position for one minute before he heard something that sounded like a voice inside the rock. After a while he heard it again. It was a goblin voice—there could be no doubt about that—and this time he could make out the words.

"Hadn't we better be moving?" it said.

A rougher and deeper voice replied, "There's no hurry. That wretched little mole won't be through tonight, if he works ever so hard. He's not by any means at the thinnest place."

"But you still think the lode does come through into our house?" said the first voice.

"Yes, but a good bit farther on than he has got to yet. If he had struck a stroke more to the side just here," said the goblin, tapping the very stone against which Curdie's head lay, "he would have been through. But he's a couple of yards past it now. Still, in case of accident, it would be as well to be getting out of this. Helfer, you'll take the great chest. That's your business."

"Yes, dad," said a third voice. "But you must help me get it on my back. It's awfully heavy, you know."

29

"Well, it isn't a bag of smoke. But you're as strong as a mountain, Helfer."

"You say so, dad. I think myself I'm all right. But I could carry ten times as much if it wasn't for my feet."

"That is your weak point, I confess, my boy."

"Ain't it yours, too, father?"

"Well, to be honest, it is a goblin weakness. Why they come so soft, I declare I haven't an idea."

"Specially when your head's so hard, you know, father."

"Yes, my boy. The goblin's glory is his head. To think how the fellows up above there have to put on helmets and things when they go fighting! Ha! ha!"

"Is that why we don't wear shoes like them, father? I think I should like it—especially when I've got a chest like that on my head."

"Well, you see, it's not the fashion. The king never wears shoes."

"The queen does," Helfer said.

"Yes, but that's for distinction. The first queen, you see—I mean the king's first wife—wore shoes, because she came from the land upstairs. When she died, the next queen would not be inferior to her, as she called it, and wore shoes, too. It was all pride. She is the hardest in forbidding them to the rest of the women."

"I'm sure I wouldn't wear them!" said the first voice, which was evidently that of the mother of the family. "I can't think why either of them should."

"Didn't I tell you the first was from upstairs?" said the father. "That was the only silly thing I ever knew His Majesty guilty of. Why should he marry an outlandish woman like that—one of our natural enemies, too? He's just as happy now with one of his own people."

"Did she die very soon? They didn't tease her to death, did they?" asked the mother.

"Oh, dear, no! The king worshiped her footmarks. She died when the young prince was born."

"How silly of her! We never do that. It must have been because she wore shoes."

"Why do they wear shoes up there?" Helfer asked.

"Ah, now that's a sensible question, son, and I will answer it. But in order to do so, I must first tell you a secret. I once saw the queen's feet."

"No! Did you? How was it?" said the other voices in unison.

"Never you mind how it was. She didn't know I saw them. And what do you think! They had toes!"

"Toes! What's that?" Helfer asked.

"You may well ask! I should never have known if I had not seen the queen's feet. Just imagine! The ends of her feet were split up into five or six thin pieces!"

"Oh, horrid! How could the king have fallen in love with her?" gasped the mother.

"You forget that she wore shoes. That is just why she wore them. That is why all the men and women upstairs wear shoes. They can't bear the sight of their own feet without them."

"Ah! now I understand. If ever you wish for shoes again, Helfer, I'll hit your feet—I will," the goblin mother said sternly.

"But, mother, with such a big box on my head—"

A horrid scream followed, which Curdie interpreted as Helfer's reply to a blow from his mother upon his feet.

"Mind you see to the bed and bedding," said the father. "As soon as we've finished our supper, we'll be up and going. Ha! ha! ha!"

"What are you laughing at, husband?"

"I'm laughing to think what a mess the miners will find themselves in—somewhere before this day ten years."

"Why, what do you mean?"

"Well, I suppose I must tell you. They're all at the palace consulting about it tonight. As soon as we've got away from this thin place I'm going there to hear what night they fix upon. I should like to see that young ruffian there on the other side, struggling in the agonies of—"

He dropped his voice so low that Curdie could hear only a growl. The growl went on in the low bass for a good while, as inarticulate as if the goblin's tongue had been a sausage. It was not until the wife spoke again that it rose to its former pitch.

"But what shall we do when you are at the palace?" she asked.

"I will see you safe in the new house I've been digging for you for the last two months. Podge, you mind the table and chairs. I commit them to your care. The table has seven legs, each chair three."

After this there arose a confused conversation about the various household goods and their transport, and Curdie heard nothing more that was of any importance.

He now knew one of the reasons for the constant sound of the goblin hammers and pickaxes at night. They were making new houses for themselves, to which they might retreat if the miners should threaten to break into their dwellings. But he had learned two things of far greater importance. The

31

first was that some grievous calamity was almost ready to fall upon the heads of the miners; the second was the one weak point of a goblin's body. He had not known that their feet were so tender as he now had reason to suspect. He had heard it said that they had no toes; he had never had opportunity to inspect them closely enough, in the dusk in which they always appeared, to satisfy himself whether it was a correct report. Indeed, he had not even been able to satisfy himself as to whether the goblins had fingers, although it was commonly said that they did not.

Although Curdie knew all the gangs and all the natural galleries in the mined part of the mountain, he had not the least idea where the palace of the king of the gnomes was. Otherwise he would have set out at once to discover the design the goblin father had mentioned. He judged, and rightly, that the palace must lie in a farther part of the mountain. If only he could get through the rock partition in time to follow the goblins as they retreated! A few blows would doubtless be sufficient—just where his ear now lay. But if he attempted to strike there with his pickax, he would only hasten the departure of the family, put them on their guard, and perhaps lose their involuntary guidance. He therefore began to feel the wall with his hands, and soon found that some of the stones were loose enough to be drawn out with little noise.

Laying hold of a large one with both his hands, he drew it gently out, and let it down softly.

"What was that noise?" said the goblin father.

Curdie blew out his light, lest it should shine through.

"It must be that one miner who stayed behind the rest," said the mother.

"No, he's been gone a good while. I haven't heard a blow for an hour. Besides, it wasn't like that."

"Then I suppose it must have been a stone carried down the brook inside."

"Perhaps. It will have more room by and by."

Curdie kept quite still for a little while. Then, hearing nothing but the sounds of their preparations for departure, and anxious to know whether the removal of the stone had made an opening into the goblins' house, he put in his hand to feel. It went in a good way, and then came in contact with something soft. He had but a moment to feel it over, it was so quickly withdrawn: it was one of the toeless goblin feet. The owner of it gave a cry of fright.

"What's the matter, Helfer?" asked his mother.

"A beast came out of the wall and licked my foot."

"Nonsense! There are no wild beasts in our country," said his father.

"But it was, father. I felt it."

"Nonsense, I say. Will you malign your native realms and reduce them to a level with the country upstairs, which is swarming with wild beasts of every description? I tell you to hold your tongue. You are no patriot."

Curdie suppressed his laughter, and lay still as a mouse—but no stiller. For every moment he kept nibbling away with his fingers at the edges of the hole. He was slowly making it bigger, because the rock had been very much shattered with the blasting.

There seemed to be a good many in the family, to judge from the mass of confused talk which now and then came through the hole. But when all were speaking together, it was not easy to make out much that was said. At length he heard once more what the father goblin was saying.

"Now, then, get your bundles on your backs. Here, Helfer, I'll help you up with your chest. Make haste. I must go to the meeting at the palace tonight!"

5   The Hall of the Goblin Palace

A sound of many soft feet followed, but soon ceased. Then Curdie flew at the hole like a tiger, and tore and pulled. The sides gave way, and it was soon large enough for him to crawl through. He would not betray himself by rekindling his lamp, but the torches of the retreating company, which he found departing up a long avenue from the door of their cave, threw back light enough to afford him a glance round the deserted home of the goblins.

To his surprise, he could discover nothing to distinguish it from an ordinary cave in the rock. The goblins had talked of coming back for the rest of their household gear; he saw nothing that would have made him suspect a family had taken shelter there for a single night.

The troop in front of him was toiling under heavy burdens. He could distinguish Helfer now and then, in the flickering light and shade, with his heavy chest on his bending shoulders. The second brother was almost buried in what looked like a great feather bed.

In a moment the troop disappeared at a turn of the way, and it was now necessary for Curdie to follow them, lest they should be around the next turning before he saw them again. He darted after them like a greyhound. When he reached the corner and looked cautiously around, he saw them again at some distance down another long passage.

He waited against this corner till they had disappeared around the next, and so followed them a long way through one passage after another. The passages grew more and more lofty, and were more and more hung with shining stalactites.

It was a strange enough procession that he followed. But the strangest part of it was the household animals that crowded amongst the feet of the goblins. It was true they had no wild animals down there, at least they did not know of any. But they had a wonderful number of tame ones, whose appearance was even more grotesque than that of their owners.

At length, turning a corner too abruptly, Curdie almost rushed into the middle of the goblin family; for they had already set down all their burdens on the floor of a cave considerably larger than that which they had left. He sprang back before anyone saw him, and retreating a good way, stood watching till the father should come out to go to the palace. Before very long, both he and his son Helfer appeared and kept on in the same direction as before, while Curdie followed them again with renewed precaution. For a long time he heard no sound except something like the rush of a river inside the rock. But at length the noise of a great shouting reached his ears. After advancing a good way farther, he thought he heard a single voice. In a moment or two, keeping after the goblins around another corner, he once more started back—this time in amazement.

He was at the entrance of a magnificent cavern of an oval shape, once probably a huge natural reservoir of water, now the great palace hall of the goblins. It rose to a tremendous height, but the roof was composed of such shining materials, and the multitude of torches carried by the goblins who crowded the floor lighted up the place so brilliantly, that Curdie could see to the top quite well. He had no idea how immense the place was until his eyes got accustomed to it, which was not for a good many minutes. The rough projections on the walls, and the shadows thrown upwards from them by the torches, made the sides of the chamber look as if they were crowded with statues that rested on brackets and pedestals.

Such a multitude of goblins filled the floor of the hall that Curdie could not help wondering whether his rhymes would be of any use. Indeed he felt considerably tempted to begin his shout of "One, two, three!" But he kept himself perfectly quiet, and peeping round the edge of the doorway, listened with both his sharp ears.

At the other end of the hall, high above the heads of the multitude, was a terracelike ledge of considerable height. Upon this sat the king and his court, the king on a throne hollowed out of a huge block of green copper ore, his court upon lower seats around it. The king had been making a speech, and the applause, which followed it, was what Curdie had heard. One of the court was now addressing the multitude.

"Hence it appears that two plans have been working together in the strong head of His Majesty for the deliverance of his people. Regardless of the fact that we were the first possessors of the upstairs regions that the sun creatures now inhabit, regardless equally of the fact that we abandoned that region for the loftiest motives, regardless also of the self-evident fact that we excel them so far in mental ability as they excel us in stature, they continue to look upon us as a degraded race, and make a mockery of all our finer feelings! But the time has almost arrived when—thanks to His Majesty's inventive genius—it will be in our power to take revenge upon them once for all."

"May it please Your Majesty—" cried a voice close by the door, which Curdie recognized as that of the goblin he had followed.

"Who is he that interrupts the chancellor?" cried another from near the throne.

"Glump," answered several voices.

"He is our trusty subject," said the king himself, in a slow and stately voice. "Let him come forward and speak."

A lane was parted through the crowd, and Glump, having ascended the platform and bowed to the king, spoke. "Sire, I would have held my peace, had I not known that only I know how near is the moment to which the chancellor has just referred. Before another day is past, the enemy will probably have broken through into my house, the partition between is now not more than a foot in thickness."

Not quite so much, thought Curdie to himself.

"This very evening I have had to remove my household effects. Therefore the sooner we are ready to carry out the plan, for which His Majesty has been making such magnificent preparations, the better. I may add that within the last few days I have perceived a small outbreak of water in my dining room, which, combined with my observations upon the course of the river escaping where the evil men enter, has convinced me that close to that spot must lie a deep gulf in its channel. This discovery will, I trust, add considerably to the otherwise immense forces at His Majesty's disposal."

He ceased, and the king graciously acknowledged his speech with a bend of his head; whereupon Glump, after a bow to His Majesty, slid down amongst the rest of the multitude.

Then the chancellor rose and resumed. "The information, which the worthy Glump has given us, might have been of considerable import at the present moment, but for that other design already referred to, which naturally takes precedence. Should His Majesty be successful in it—as who dares to doubt?—then a peace, all to the advantage of the goblin kingdom, will be established for a generation at least, rendered absolutely secure by the pledge which His Royal Highness the prince will have and hold for the good behavior of her relatives. Should His Majesty fail—which who shall dare even to imagine in his most secret thoughts?—then will be the time for carrying out with rigor the design to which Glump referred, and for which our preparations are even now all but completed."

Curdie did not understand all of the chancellor's words, and wished the goblin plans had been stated plainly. But perceiving that the assembly was drawing to a close and that there was little chance of either plan being revealed more fully, he thought it prudent to make his escape, and so he slipped away.

There was not much danger of meeting any goblins, for all the men were behind him in the palace. But there was considerable danger of his taking a wrong turn, for he now had no light, and had therefore to depend upon his memory and his hands.

He was most anxious to get back through the hole before the goblins should return to fetch the remains of their furniture. It was not that he was in the least afraid of them, but, as it was of the utmost importance that he should discover what their plans were, he must not allow them the least suspicion that they were watched by a miner.

He hurried on, feeling his way along the walls of rock. Had he not been very courageous, he would have been very anxious, for he must have known that if he lost his way it would be the most difficult thing in the world to find it again. Well might he wish that he had brought his lamp and tinderbox with him. He had not thought of them when he crept so eagerly after the goblins!

He wished it all the more when, after a while, he found his way blocked up, and could get no farther. It was of no use to turn back, for he had not the least idea where he had begun to go wrong. Mechanically, he moved his hands about on the walls that hemmed him in. One hand came upon a place where a tiny stream of water was running down the face of the rock.

What a stupid I am! he said to himself. _I am actually at the end of my journey! And here are the goblins coming back to fetch their things!_ he added, as the red glimmer of their torches appeared at the end of the long avenue that led up to the cave.

In a moment he had thrown himself on the floor, and wriggled backwards through the hole. It was all he could do to lift the largest stone he had taken out of the hole, but he did manage to shove it in place again. He sat down on the ore heap to think.

He was fairly sure that the goblins' second plan was to flood the mine by breaking outlets for the water accumulated in the natural reservoirs of the mountain. While the part hollowed by the miners had remained shut off from that inhabited by the goblins, they had had no opportunity to harm the miners. But now that a passage was broken through, and the goblins' part proved the higher in the mountain, it was clear to Curdie that the mine could be destroyed in an hour. Water was always the chief danger to which the miners were exposed.

It seemed to Curdie that it would be best to build up the whole of this gang, filling it with stone and clay or lime, so that there should be no channel for the water to get into. There was not immediate danger, for the execution of the goblins' plan was contingent upon the failure of that first, unknown design. Curdie was most anxious to keep the door of communication open, that he might, if possible, discover what the former plan was.

As soon as Curdie found that the goblins had again departed, he lighted his lamp, and proceeded to fill the hole he had made with such stones as he could withdraw again later. He then thought it better to go home and have some sleep, as he might have occasion to be up a good many nights after this.

How pleasant the night air felt upon the outside of the mountain after what he had gone through inside it! He hurried up the hill without meeting a single goblin on the way, and called and tapped at the window until he woke his father, who soon rose and let him in. He told him the whole story, and, just as he had expected, his father thought it best to work that lode no farther, but at the same time to pretend occasionally to be at work there, so the goblins might have no suspicions.

6   The Old Lady's Room

The weather continued fine for weeks, and the little princess went out every day. The only uncomfortable thing was that her nurse was so nervous and particular about being in before the sun was down that often she would take to her heels when nothing worse than a fleecy cloud crossing the sun threw a shadow on the hillside. Many an evening they were home a full hour before the sunlight had left the weathercock on the stables. If it had not been for such odd behavior, Irene would by this time have almost forgotten the goblins.

One splendid, sunshiny day, Irene, who was playing on a lawn in the garden, heard the distant blast of a bugle. She jumped up with a cry of joy, for she knew by that particular blast that her father was on his way to see her. She shaded her eyes with her hand and looked far away to catch the first glimpse of shining armor.

In a few moments a little troop came glittering round the shoulder of a hill. Spears and helmets were sparkling and gleaming, banners were flying, horses prancing. Again came the bugle blast, which was to her like the voice of her father calling across the distance: "Irene, I'm coming."

On and on they came until she could clearly distinguish the king on his white horse, taller than any of the men with him. He wore a narrow circle of gold set with jewels around his helmet. As he came still nearer, Irene could discern the flashing of the stones in the sun. It was a long time since he had been to see her, and her little heart beat faster and faster as the shining troop approached, for she loved her king-papa very dearly and was nowhere so happy as in his arms. She ran to the gate, and stood there till up they came clanging up and stamping with one more bright bugle blast, which said: "Irene, I am come."

When the horsemen pulled up, Irene ran to the side of the white horse and held up her arms. The king stooped and took her hands. In an instant she was on the saddle and clasped in his great, strong arms. He had gentle, blue eyes, but a nose that made him look like an eagle. A long, dark beard, streaked with silvery lines, flowed from his mouth almost to his waist, and as Irene sat on the saddle and hid her glad face upon his bosom it mingled with her golden hair.

After he had held her to his heart for a minute he spoke to his white horse. The great, beautiful creature, which had been prancing so proudly a little while before, walked as gently as a lady through the gate and up to the door of the house. Then the king set Irene on the ground and, dismounting, took her hand and walked with her into the great hall, which was hardly ever entered except when he came to see his little princess. There he sat down, with two of his councillors who had accompanied him, to have some refreshment. Irene sat on his right hand.

After the king had eaten and drunk, he turned to the princess and said, stroking her hair, "Now, my child, what shall we do next?"

This was the question he almost always put to her first after their meal together. Irene had been waiting for it with some impatience, for now, she thought, she should be able to settle a question which constantly perplexed her.

"I should like you to take me to see my great old grandmother."

The king looked grave. "What does my little daughter mean?"

"I mean the Queen Irene that lives up in the tower—the very old lady, you know, with the long hair of silver."

The king only gazed at his little princess with a look that she could not understand.

"You know she's up there, don't you?" Irene went on.

"No," said the king, very quietly.

"Then it must all be a dream. I half thought it was, but I couldn't be sure. Now I am sure of it. Besides, I couldn't find her the next time I went up."

At that moment a snow-white pigeon flew in at an open window and settled upon Irene's head. She broke into a merry laugh, cowered a little, and put up her hands to her head.

The king stretched out his hand to take the pigeon, but it spread its wings and flew again through the open window, where its whiteness made one flash in the sun and vanished.

The king laid his hand on his princess's head and held it back a little. He gazed in her face, smiled half a smile, and sighed half a sigh. "Come, my child; we'll have a walk in the garden together."

"You won't come up and see my huge, great, beautiful grandmother, then, king-papa?"

"Not this time," said the king very gently. "She has not invited me, you know, and great old ladies like her do not choose to be visited without permission asked and given."

The garden was a very lovely place. Being upon a mountainside, there were parts in it where the rocks came through in great masses. Tufts of heather grew upon them, while nearby would be lovely roses and lilies and other pleasant garden flowers, a mingling of the wild mountain with the civilized garden.

Against one of these rocks was a garden seat, shadowed from the afternoon sun by the overhanging of the rock itself. There Irene and her king-papa sat because the sun was hot; and there they talked together of many things.

At length the king said, "You were out late one evening, Irene."

"Yes, papa. It was my fault; and Lootie was very sorry."

"I must talk to Lootie about it."

"Don't speak loudly to her, please, papa. She's been so afraid of being late ever since! Indeed she has not been naughty. It was only a mistake for once."

"Once might be too often," murmured the king to himself, as he stroked his child's head.

He sat for a good while thinking. Then he rose and, leaving Irene where she was, went into the house and sent for Lootie, with whom he had a talk that made her cry.

When in the evening he rode away upon his great white horse, he left six of his attendants behind him, with orders that three of them should watch outside the house every night, walking round and round it from sunset to sunrise. It was clear he was not quite comfortable about the princess.

The autumn came and went by. There were no more flowers in the garden. The wind blew strong, and howled among the rocks. The rain fell, and drenched the few yellow and red leaves that could not get off the bare branches. Again and again there would be a glorious morning followed by a pouring afternoon, and sometimes, for a week together, there would be rain, nothing but rain, all day.

The winter drew on, and the princess found things growing dreary. When it was too stormy to go out, and she had got tired of her toys, Lootie would take her about the house, sometimes to the housekeeper's room, where the housekeeper made much of her; sometimes to the servants' hall or the kitchen, where she was not princess merely, but absolute queen, and ran a great risk of being spoiled. Sometimes Irene would run off herself to the room where the men-at-arms whom the king had left sat, and they showed her their armaments and did what they could to amuse her. Still at times she found it very dreary, and often wished that her huge great-grandmother had not been a dream.

One morning the nurse left her with the housekeeper for a while. To amuse her the housekeeper turned out the contents of an old cabinet upon the table. The little princess found treasures, queer and ancient ornaments, and many things the use of which she could not imagine, to be far more interesting than her own toys, and sat playing with them for two hours or more. But, at length, in handling a curious old-fashioned brooch, she ran the pin of it into her thumb. She gave a little scream with the sharpness of the pain, but would have thought little more of it had not the pain increased and her thumb begun to swell.

This alarmed the housekeeper greatly. The nurse was fetched; the doctor was sent for. Her hand was poulticed, and long before her usual time the princess was put to bed. The pain still continued; and although she fell asleep and dreamed a good many dreams, the pain was always in every dream. At last it woke her up.

The moon was shining brightly into the room. The poultice had fallen off her hand and the thumb was burning hot. She fancied if she could hold it into the moonlight that would cool it. So she got out of bed, without waking the nurse, who lay at the other end of the room, and went to the window. When she looked out she saw one of the men-at-arms walking in the garden with the moonlight glancing off his armor. She was just going to tap on the window and call him, when she realized that might wake Lootie, who would put her into her bed again. So she resolved to go to the window of another room, and call him from there.

She opened the door very gently and went through the nursery, which did not look into the garden, to go to the other window. But when she came to the foot of the old staircase, there was the moon shining down from some window high up, making the worm-eaten oak look very strange and delicate and lovely. In a moment she was putting her feet one after the other in the silvery path up the stair, looking behind as she went to see the shadow they made in the middle of the silver. Some little girls would have been afraid to find themselves thus alone in the middle of the night, but Irene was a princess.

As she went slowly up the stair, not quite sure that she was not dreaming, suddenly a great longing rose up in her heart to find the old lady with the silvery hair.

"If she is a dream," she said to herself, "then I am likelier to find her, if I am dreaming."

So up and up she went, stair after stair, until she came to the many rooms, all just as she had seen them before. As if she had known every step of the way, she walked straight to the door at the foot of the narrow stair that led to the tower.

"What if I should really find my beautiful old grandmother up there!" she said to herself as she crept up the steep steps.

When she reached the top, she stood a moment listening in the dark. Yes! It was the hum of the spinning wheel! What a diligent grandmother to work both day and night!

She tapped gently at the door.

"Come in, Irene," said the sweet voice.

The princess opened the door and entered. In the middle of the moonlight sat the old lady in her black dress with the white lace, her silvery hair mingling with the moonlight.

"Come in, Irene," she said again. "Can you tell me what I am spinning?"

She speaks, thought Irene, *just as if she had seen me five minutes ago, or yesterday at the farthest.* "No," she answered. "I don't know what you are spinning. Please, I thought you were a dream. Why couldn't I find you before, great-great-grandmother?"

"That you are hardly old enough to understand. But you would have found me sooner if you hadn't come to think I was a dream. I will give you one reason, though, why you couldn't find me. I didn't want you to find me."

"Why, please?"

"Because I did not want Lootie to know I was here."

"But you told me to tell Lootie."

"Yes. But I knew Lootie would not believe you. If she were to see me sitting here, she wouldn't believe me, either."

"Why?"

"Because she couldn't. She would rub her eyes, and go away and say she felt

46

queer, and forget half of it and more, and then say it had been all a dream."

"Just like me," said Irene, feeling very much ashamed of herself.

"Yes, but not just like you; for you've come again. Lootie wouldn't have come again. She would have said she had had enough of such nonsense."

"Is it naughty of Lootie, then?"

"It would be naughty of you. I've never done anything for Lootie."

"And you did wash my face and hands for me," said Irene, beginning to cry.

The old lady smiled a sweet smile. "I'm not vexed with you, my child—nor with Lootie either. But I don't want you to say anything more to Lootie about me. If she should ask you, you must just be silent."

All the time they talked the old lady kept on spinning.

"You haven't told me yet what I am spinning," she said.

"Because I don't know. It's very pretty stuff."

It was indeed very pretty stuff. There was a good bunch of it on the distaff attached to the spinning wheel, and in the moonlight it shone like silver, but shone gray rather than white, and glittered only a little. And the thread the old lady drew out from it was so fine that Irene could hardly see it.

"I am spinning this for you, my child."

"For me! What am I to do with it, please?"

"I will tell you by and by. But first I will tell you what it is. It is spiderwebs—of a particular kind. My pigeons bring it to me from over the great sea. There is only one forest where the spiders live who make this particular kind—the finest and strongest of any. I have nearly finished my present job. What is on the rock now will be enough. I have a week's work there yet, though," she added, looking at the bunch.

"Do you work all day and all night, too, great-great-great-great-grandmother?" said the princess, thinking to be very polite with so many greats.

"I am not quite so great as all that," she answered, smiling almost merrily. "If you call me grandmother, that will do. No, I don't work every night—only moonlit nights, and then no longer than the moon shines upon my wheel. I shan't work much longer tonight."

"And what will you do next, grandmother?"

"Go to bed. Would you like to see my bedroom?"

"Yes, that I should."

The old lady rose, and left her wheel standing just as it was. Then she took Irene by the hand, but it was her bad hand, and Irene gave a little cry of pain.

"My child!" said her grandmother, "what is the matter?"

Irene held her hand into the moonlight, so the old lady might see it, and told her all about it, at which she looked grave. But she only said: "Give me your other hand," and, having led her out upon the dark landing, opened the door on the opposite side of it. Much to Irene's surprise she saw the loveliest room she had ever seen in her life! It was large and lofty, and dome-shaped. From the center hung a lamp as round as a ball, shining as if with the brightest moonlight, which made everything visible in the room, though not so clearly that the princess could tell what many of the things were. A large oval bed stood in the middle, with a coverlet of rose color, and velvet curtains all around it of a lovely pale blue. The walls were also blue, spangled all over with what looked like stars of silver.

The old lady left her and, going to a strange-looking cabinet, opened it and took out a curious silver casket. Then she sat down on a low chair and, calling Irene, made her kneel before her while she looked at her hand. Having examined it, she opened the casket, and took from it a little ointment. The sweetest odor filled the room—like that of roses and lilies—as she rubbed the ointment gently all over the hot, swollen hand. Her touch was so pleasant and cool that it seemed to drive away the pain and heat wherever it came.

"Oh, grandmother! It is so nice!" said Irene. "Thank you; thank you."

Then the old lady went to a chest of drawers, and took out a large handkerchief of gossamerlike cambric, which she tied round her hand.

"I don't think I can let you go away tonight. Would you like to sleep with me?"

"Oh, yes, yes, dear grandmother!" Irene would have clapped her hands, forgetting that she could not.

Then the old lady got a large silver basin, and having poured some water into it made Irene sit on the chair, and washed her feet. This done, she was ready for bed. And oh, what a delicious bed it was into which her grandmother laid her! She hardly could have told she was lying upon anything; she felt nothing but the softness. The old lady lay down beside her.

"Why don't you put out your moon?" asked the princess.

"That never goes out, night or day. In the darkest night, if any of my pigeons are out on a message, they always see my moon and know where to fly to."

"But if somebody besides the pigeons were to see it—somebody about the house, I mean—they would come to look what it was and find you."

"The better for them, then," said the old lady. "But it does not happen above five times in a hundred years. The greater part of those who do see it take it for a meteor, wink their eyes, and forget it again. Besides, nobody could find the

room except I pleased. I will tell you a secret. If that light were to go out, you would fancy yourself lying in a bare garret, on a heap of old straw, and would not see one of the pleasant things round about you.''

"I hope it will never go out.'' The little princess nestled close up to the old lady, who took her in both her arms and held her close.

"Oh, dear! this is so nice!'' said the princess. "I should like to lie here forever.''

"You may if you will,'' said the old lady. "But first I must put you to one trial—not a *very* hard one, I hope. A week from this night you must come back to me. If you don't, I do not know when you may find me again, and you will soon want me very much.''

"Oh! please, don't let me forget.''

"You shall not forget. The only question is whether you will believe I am anywhere, whether you will believe I am anything but a dream. You may be sure I will do all I can to help you to come. But it will rest with you after all.''

"I *will* try.''

"Then good night,'' said the old lady.

In a moment more the little princess was dreaming of summer seas and moonlight and mossy springs, of great, murmuring trees and beds of wild flowers.

In the morning she found herself in her own bed. There was no handkerchief or anything else on her hand, only a sweet odor lingering about it. The swelling had all gone down; the prick of the brooch had vanished. In fact, her hand was perfectly well.

7 The Cobs' Creatures

Curdie spent many nights in the mine. His father and he had taken Mrs. Peterson into the secret, for they knew mother could hold her tongue. But Curdie did not tell her that every night he spent in the mine, part of it went in earning a new red petticoat for her.

When left alone in the mine, Curdie always worked on for an hour or two at first, following the lode which led into the deserted goblin habitation. After that, he would set out on a reconnoitering expedition. In order to manage this, or rather the return from it, better than the first time, he had bought a huge ball of fine string. The end of this string he fastened to his pickax, which figured no bad anchor. Then, with the ball in his hand, unrolling it as he went, he would set out in the dark through the natural gangs of the goblins' territory.

The first night or two he came upon nothing worth remembering. But at length, I think on the third or fourth night, he found a company of the best sappers and miners amongst the goblins, hard at work. What were they about? He lurked and watched, but without success. He had again and again to retreat in haste, a proceeding rendered the more difficult in that he had to gather up his string as he returned upon its course. It was not that he was afraid of the goblins, but that he was afraid of their finding out that they were watched.

When he reached home towards morning, his haste sometimes had to be such that his string—for lack of time to wind it up as he "dodged the cobs"—would be in what seemed a hopeless entanglement. But after a good, though short, sleep, he always found his mother had it right again. There it was, wound in a most respectable ball, ready for use the moment he should want it!

"I can't think how you do it, mother."

"I follow the thread," she would answer, "just as you do in the mine."

About this time the gentlemen whom the king had left behind him to watch over the princess each had occasion to doubt his own eyes, for very strange were the creatures to which those eyes would bear witness. They were so grotesque and misshapen as to be more like a child's drawings upon his slate than anything natural. The men-at-arms saw them only at night, while on guard about the house. The testimony of the man who first reported having seen one of them was that, as he was walking slowly round the house, he caught sight of a creature standing on its hind legs in the moonlight, with its forefeet upon a window ledge, staring in at the window.

Its body might have been that of a dog or wolf, he thought, but he declared on his honor that its head was twice the size it ought to have been, and as round as a ball, while the face, which it turned upon him as it fled, was more like one carved by a boy upon a turnip than anything else he could think of. He sent an arrow after it, and thought he must have struck it; for it gave an unearthly howl.

The other men-at-arms laughed at him, and said he must have taken too long a pull at the ale jug. But before two nights were over he had someone to side with him, for another had seen something strange. The description the second man gave of the creature was even yet more grotesque and unlikely. They were both laughed at by the rest; but every night another came over to their side, until at last there was only one left to laugh at all his companions. Two nights more passed, and he saw nothing; but on the third he came rushing from the garden to the other two before the house in agitation.

Running with him into that part of the garden which I have already described, all three men saw a score of creatures, not one of which was like another, hideous and ludicrous at once, gamboling on the lawn in the moonlight. The noises they made, although not loud, were as uncouth and varied as their forms, and could be described neither as squeaks nor roars nor howls nor barks nor yells nor screams nor croaks nor hisses nor mews nor shrieks, but only as something like all of them mingled in one horrible dissonance.

Keeping in the shade, the watchers had a few moments to recover them-

selves before the hideous creatures suspected their presence; but all at once, as if by common consent, they scampered off in the direction of a great rock, and vanished.

They were, of course, household animals belonging to the goblins, whose ancestors had taken their ancestors many centuries before from the upper regions of light into the lowest regions of darkness. The original stocks of these horrible creatures were very much the same as the animals now seen about farms and homes in the country, with the exception of a few wild creatures, which the goblins had caught when young and tamed. In the course of time all had undergone even greater changes than had passed upon their owners. Their descendants had altered into such creatures as I have not attempted to describe except in the vaguest manner, the various parts of their bodies assuming the most abnormal developments. But what increased the gruesomeness tenfold was that, from constant association with the goblins, the creatures' countenances had grown in grotesque resemblance to the human.

These animals had begun to show themselves about the king's country house because they had discovered a passage that led out of the earth. In the course of the goblins' tunneling they had broken into the channel of a small stream to the outside. Some of the creatures, hovering as they often did about their masters, had found the hole, and had, with curiosity which had grown to a passion, proceeded to explore the channel. The stream was the same that ran out by the seat on which Irene and her king-papa had sat at his last visit, and the goblin creatures found it jolly fun to get out for a romp on a smooth lawn such as they had never seen in all their poor, miserable lives.

For several nights after the men-at-arms had all agreed about the fact of the visits of some horrible creatures, they watched with special attention that part of the garden. Perhaps indeed they gave, in consequence, too little attention to the house.

8　The Very Next Week

During the whole of the week Irene had been thinking every other moment of her promise to the old lady, although even now she could not feel quite sure that she had not been dreaming. Could it really be that an old lady lived up in the top of the house, with pigeons and a spinning wheel and a lamp that never went out? She was, however, nonetheless determined to ascend the three stairs on the coming Friday, walk through the passages with the many doors, and try to find the tower in which she had either seen or dreamed her grandmother.

At length the longed-for day arrived, and lest Lootie should be moved to watch her too closely, Irene endeavored to keep herself as well behaved as possible. In the afternoon she asked for her doll's house, and went on arranging and rearranging the various rooms and their inhabitants for a whole hour. Then she gave a sigh and threw herself back in her chair. One of the dolls would not sit, and another would not stand, and they were all very tiresome. Besides it was now getting dark, and the darker it got the more excited Irene became.

"I see you want your tea, princess," said the nurse. "I will go and get it. The room feels close, so I will open the window a little. The evening is mild; it won't hurt you."

"There's no fear of that, Lootie," said Irene, wishing the nurse had put off going for the tea till it was darker, when she might have made her escape.

I fancy Lootie was longer in returning that she had intended, for when Irene, who had been lost in thought, looked up, she saw it was nearly dark. At the same moment she caught sight of a pair of eyes, bright with a green light, glowering at her through the open window. The next instant something leaped into the room. It was like a cat, with legs as long as a horse's, but its body no bigger and its legs no thicker than those of a cat. Irene was too frightened to cry out, but not too frightened to jump from her chair and run from the room.

It is plain enough to every one of my readers what she ought to have done—and indeed Irene thought of it herself. But when she came to the foot of the old stair, just outside the nursery door, she imagined the creature running up those long flights after her, and pursuing her through the dark passages—which, after all, might not lead to a tower! That thought was too much. Her heart failed her, and, turning from the stair, she rushed along to the hall, whence, finding the front door open, she darted into the court pursued—at least she thought so—by the creature.

No one happening to see her, on she ran, straight out of the gate and up the mountain. It was foolish indeed, thus to run farther and farther from all who could help her, as if she had been seeking a fit spot for the goblin creature to eat her at his leisure.

The princess was soon out of breath with running uphill. But she ran on, for she fancied the horrible creature just behind her, forgetting that such long legs as those would have overtaken her long ago. At last she could run no longer, and fell, unable even to scream, by the roadside. She lay for some time half dead with terror. But finding nothing lay hold of her, and her breath beginning to come back, she ventured at length to get up and peer anxiously about her.

It was now so dark she could see nothing. Not a single star was out. She could not even tell in what direction the house lay, and between her and home she fancied the dreadful creature lying ready to pounce upon her. She saw now that she ought to have run up the stairs at once. It was well she did not scream; for, although very few of the goblins had come out for weeks, a stray idler or two might have heard her. She sat down upon a stone, and nobody but one who had done something wrong could have been more miserable.

A raindrop fell on her face. She looked up, and for a moment her terror was lost in astonishment. A great silvery globe was hanging in the air; and as she gazed at the lovely thing, her courage revived. What could that light be? What if it should be—yes—it must be her great-great-grandmother's lamp, which

guided her pigeons home through the darkest night! She jumped up; she had but to keep that light in view and she must find the house.

Her heart grew strong. Speedily, yet softly, she walked down the hill, hoping to pass the watching creature unseen. Dark as it was, there was now little danger of choosing the wrong road. And by looking at the lamp and then dropping her eyes, she could see the road for a yard or two in front of her, and this saved her from several falls, for the road was very rough.

But all at once, to her dismay, the light vanished, and the terror of the beast again laid hold of her heart. The same instant, however, she caught sight of the light of the windows, and knew exactly where she was. It was too dark to run, but she made what haste she could, and reached the gate in safety. She found the house door still open, ran through the hall, and, without even looking into the nursery, bounded straight up the stair, and the next, and the next; then turning to the right, ran through the long avenue of silent rooms, and found her way at once to the door at the foot of the tower stair.

When first the nurse missed her, she fancied she was playing her a trick and for some time took no trouble about her. But at last, getting frightened, she had begun to search; and when the princess entered, the whole household was running hither and thither over the house, hunting for her. A few seconds after she reached the stair of the tower, they had even begun to search the neglected rooms. But by this time she was knocking at the old lady's door.

"Come in, Irene," said the silvery voice of her grandmother.

The princess opened the door and peeped in. But the room was quite dark and there was no sound of the spinning wheel. She grew frightened once more, thinking that, although the room was there, the old lady might be a dream after all. She remembered, however, that at night she spun only in the moonlight, and concluded that must be why there was no sweet, beelike humming. Before she had time to think another thought, she heard the voice again, saying as before, "Come in, Irene."

From the sound, she understood at once that the old lady was not in the room beside her. Perhaps she was in her bedroom. She turned across the passage, feeling her way to the other door, opened it, and went in. Oh, what a lovely haven to reach from the darkness and fear through which she had come! The soft light made her feel as if she were going into the heart of the milkiest pearl.

"I've lighted a fire for you, Irene. You're cold and wet," said her grandmother.

Then Irene looked again, and saw that what she had taken for a huge bouquet of red roses on a low stand against the wall was in fact a fire, which burned in the shapes of the loveliest and reddest roses, glowing gorgeously between the heads and wings of two cherubs of shining silver. And when she came nearer, she found that the smell of roses with which the room was filled came from the fire-roses on the hearth.

Her grandmother was dressed in the loveliest pale blue velvet, over which her hair, no longer white, but of a rich golden color, streamed like a cataract. It flowed from under the edge of a circle of shining silver, set with alternated pearls and opals. Her face was that of a woman of three-and-twenty.

The princess was so bewildered with astonishment and admiration that she drew nigh with timidity, feeling dirty and uncomfortable. The lady was seated on a low chair by the side of the fire, with hands outstretched to take her, but the princess hung back with a troubled smile.

"Why, what's the matter?" asked her grandmother. "You haven't been doing anything wrong—I know that by your face, though it is rather miserable. What's the matter, my dear?"

And she still held out her arms.

"Dear grandmother," said Irene, "I'm not so sure that I haven't done something wrong. I ought to have run up to you at once when the long-legged cat came in at the window, instead of running out on the mountain."

"You were taken by surprise, my child, and are not so likely to do it again. It is when people do wrong things willfully that they are the more likely to do them again. Come to me."

"But, grandmother, you're so beautiful and grand with your crown on! And I am so dirty with mud and rain! I should quite spoil your beautiful blue dress."

With a merry little laugh the lady sprang from her chair, caught the child to her, and, kissing the tearstained face over and over, sat down with her in her lap.

"Oh, grandmother! You'll make yourself such a mess!"

"You darling! Do you think I care more for my dress than for my little girl? Besides, look here."

As she spoke she set her down, and Irene saw to her dismay that the lovely dress was covered with the mud from her fall on the mountain road. But the lady stooped to the fire, and taking from it one of the burning roses by its stalk, passed it once and again and a third time over the front of her dress. When Irene looked, not a single stain was to be discovered.

"There!" said her grandmother. "You won't mind coming to me now?"

But Irene again hung back, eyeing the flaming rose that the lady held in her hand.

"You're not afraid of the rose, are you?" she said, about to throw it on the hearth again.

"Oh! Don't, please!" cried Irene. "Won't you hold it to my frock and my hands and my face? And I'm afraid my feet and my knees want it, too!"

"No," answered her grandmother, smiling a little sadly, as she threw the rose from her. "It is too hot for you yet. It would set your frock in a flame. Besides, I don't want to make you clean tonight. I want your nurse and the rest of the people to see you as you are, for you will have to tell them how you ran away for fear of the long-legged cat. I should like to wash you, but they would not believe you then."

"Very well, grandmother," answered Irene, and was again silent for some moments thinking. Then she said: "How was it, grandmother, that I saw your beautiful lamp—not the light of it only—but the great, round, silvery lamp itself, hanging alone in the great open air, high up? It was your lamp I saw, wasn't it?"

"Yes, my child. It was my lamp."

"Then how was it? I don't see a window."

"When I please I can make the lamp shine through the walls, shine so strong that it melts them away from before the sight, and shows itself as you saw it. But, as I told you, not everybody can see it."

"How is it that I can, then?"

"It is a gift born with you. And one day I hope everybody will have it. But," added the lady, rising, "you must sit in my chair while I get you the present I have been preparing for you. I told you my spinning was for you. It is finished now, and I am going to fetch it. I have been keeping it warm under one of my brooding pigeons."

Irene sat down in the low chair, and her grandmother left her, shutting the door behind her. The child sat gazing, now at the rose fire, now at the starry walls, now at the silver light, and a great quietness grew in her heart. If all the long-legged cats in the world had come rushing at her she would not have been afraid of them for a moment.

She had been gazing at the lovely lamp for some minutes fixedly. Turning her eyes, she found the wall had vanished, for she was looking out on the dark, cloudy night. But though she heard the wind blowing, none of it blew upon her. In a moment more, the clouds themselves parted, or rather vanished like the wall, and she looked straight into the stars, flashing gloriously in the dark blue. It was but for a moment. The clouds gathered again and shut out the stars; the wall gathered again and shut out the clouds; and there stood the lady

60

beside her with the loveliest smile on her face, and a shimmering ball in her hand, about the size of a pigeon's egg.

"There, Irene; there is my work for you!" she said, holding out the ball to the princess.

Irene took it in her hand, and looked at it all over. It sparkled a little, and shone here and there, but not much. It was of a sort of gray white, something like spun glass.

"Is this all your spinning, grandmother?"

"All since you came to the house. There is more there than you think."

"How pretty it is! What am I to do with it, please?"

"That I will now explain to you," answered the lady, turning from her and going to her cabinet.

She came back with a small ring in her hand. Then she took the ball from Irene's, and did something with them—Irene could not tell what.

"Give me your hand," she said.

Irene held up her right hand.

"Yes, that is the hand I want," said the lady, and put the ring on the forefinger of it.

"What a beautiful ring!" said Irene. "What is the stone called?"

"It is a fire opal."

"Please, am I to keep it?"

"Always."

"Oh, grandmother, I will take such care of it! But—" she added, hesitating.

"But what?"

"What am I to say when Lootie asks me where I got it?"

"You will ask her where you got it," answered the lady, smiling.

"I don't see how I can do that."

"You will, though. But don't trouble yourself about it. You will see when the time comes."

So saying, the lady turned, and threw the little ball into the rose fire.

"Oh, grandmother!" exclaimed Irene. "I thought you had spun it for me. Now it's burnt in the fire!"

The lady put her hand in the fire, brought out the ball, glimmering as before, and held it towards her. Irene stretched out her hand to take it, but the lady turned and, going to her cabinet, opened a drawer, and laid the ball in it.

"Have I done anything to vex you, grandmother?" said Irene pitifully.

"No, my darling. But you must understand that no one ever gives anything to another properly and really without keeping it. That ball is yours."

"Oh! I'm not to take it with me! You are going to keep it for me!"

"You are to take it with you. I've fastened the end of it to the ring on your finger."

Irene looked at the ring. "I can't see it there, grandmother."

"Feel—a little way from the ring—towards the cabinet," said the lady.

"Oh! I do feel it!" exclaimed the princess. "But I can't see it."

"No. The thread is too fine for you to see it. Now you can fancy how much spinning that took, although it does seem such a little ball."

"But what use can I make of it, if it lies in your cabinet?"

"That is what I will explain to you. Now listen. If ever you find yourself in any danger—such, for example, as you were in this evening—you must take off your ring and put it under the pillow of your bed. Then you must lay your forefinger, the same that wore the ring, upon the thread, and follow the thread wherever it leads you."

"Oh, how delightful! It will lead me to you, grandmother, I know!"

"Yes. But, remember, it may seem to you a very roundabout way indeed, and you must not doubt the thread. Of one thing you may be sure, that while you hold it, I hold it, too."

"It is very wonderful! But," said Irene, still puzzled, "won't the thread get in somebody's way and be broken, if the one end is fast to my ring and the other laid in your cabinet?"

"You will find all that will arrange itself. I am afraid it is time for you to go. Everybody in the house is miserable about you, and it would be cruel to keep them so all night. You must go downstairs."

"I'm so glad you didn't say 'Go home,' for this is my home. Mayn't I call this my home?"

"You may, my child. And I trust you will always think it your home. Now come. I must take you back without anyone seeing you."

"Please, I want to ask you one question more. Is it because you have your crown on that you look so young?"

"No, child," answered her grandmother. "It is because I felt so young this evening that I put my crown on. And I thought you would like to see your old grandmother in her best."

"Why do you call yourself old? You're not old, grandmother."

"I am very old indeed. It is so silly of people to fancy that old age means crookedness and witheredness and feebleness and sticks and spectacles and rheumatism and forgetfulness! Old age has nothing whatever to do with all that. The right old age means strength and beauty and mirth and courage and clear eyes and strong, painless limbs. I am older than you are able to think, and—"

"And look at you, grandmother!" cried Irene, jumping up and flinging her arms about her neck. "I won't be so silly again, I promise you. I wish I were as old as you, grandmother. I don't think you are ever afraid of anything."

"Not for long, at least, my child. Perhaps by the time I am two thousand years of age, I shall never be afraid of anything. But I confess I have sometimes been afraid about my children—sometimes about you, Irene."

"Oh, I'm *so* sorry, grandmother! Tonight, I suppose, you mean."

"Yes, a little tonight. But a good deal when you had all but made up your mind that I was a dream, and no real great-great-grandmother. You must not suppose I am blaming you for that. I daresay you could not help it."

"I don't know, grandmother," said the princess, beginning to cry. "I can't always do myself as I should like. And I don't always try. I'm very sorry anyhow."

The lady stooped, lifted her in her arms, and sat down with her in her chair, holding her close. In a few minutes the princess had sobbed herself to sleep. How long she slept, I do not know. When she came to herself she was sitting in her own high chair at the nursery table, with her doll's house before her.

9   The Ring

The same moment her nurse came into the room, sobbing. When she saw Irene sitting there, she started back with a loud cry of amazement and joy. Then running to her, she caught her in her arms and covered her with kisses.

"My precious, darling princess! Where have you been? What has happened to you? We've all been crying our eyes out, and searching the house from top to bottom for you."

"Oh, Lootie! I've had such a dreadful adventure!" she replied, and told her all about the cat with the long legs, and how she ran out upon the mountain, and came back again. But she said nothing of her grandmother or her lamp.

"And there we've been searching for you all over the house for more than an hour and a half!" exclaimed the nurse. "But that's no matter, now we've got you! Only, princess, I must say," she added, her mood changing, "what you ought to have done was to call for your own Lootie to come and help you, instead of running out of the house, and up the mountain, in that wild, foolish fashion."

"Well, Lootie," said Irene quietly, "perhaps if you had a big cat, all legs, running at you, you mightn't exactly know what was the wisest thing to do at the moment. When those creatures came at you that night on the mountain, you were so frightened yourself that you lost your way home."

This put a stop to Lootie's reproaches. She had been on the point of saying that the long-legged cat must have been a twilight fancy of the princess's, but the memory of the horrors of that night, and of the talking-to which the king had given her in consequence, prevented her.

Without another word she went and got some fresh tea and bread and butter for the princess. Before she returned, the whole household, headed by the housekeeper, burst into the nursery to exult over their darling. The gentlemen-at-arms followed, and were ready enough to believe all she told them about the long-legged cat. In their own hearts they blamed themselves for not having kept better watch. They redoubled their vigilance, and for some time there was no further cause of alarm.

When the princess woke the next morning, her nurse was bending over her.

"How your ring does glow this morning, princess! Just like a fiery rose!" she said.

"Does it, Lootie?" returned Irene. "Who gave me the ring, Lootie? I know I've had it a long time, but where did I get it? I don't remember."

"I think it must have been your mother gave it to you, princess. But really, for as long as you have worn it, I don't remember that ever I heard."

"I will ask my king-papa the next time he comes."

The spring so dear to all creatures, young and old, came at last. Before the first few days of it had gone, the king rode through its budding valleys to see his little daughter. He had been in a distant part of his dominions all the winter, for he moved from place to place so that all his people might know him. Wherever he journeyed, he kept a constant lookout for the ablest and best men to put into office; and wherever he found himself mistaken, and those he had appointed incapable or unjust, he removed them at once. It was his care of the people that kept him from seeing his princess so often as he would have liked.

Once more Irene heard the bugle blast, and once more she was at the gate to meet her father as he rode up on his great white horse.

After they had been alone for a little while, she thought of what she had resolved to ask him.

"Please, king-papa," she said, "will you tell me where I got this pretty ring? I can't remember."

The king looked at it. A strange, beautiful smile spread like sunshine over his face. "It was your queen-mama's once," he said.

"And why isn't it hers now?"

"She does not want it now," said the king, looking grave.

"Why doesn't she want it now?"

"Because she's gone where all those rings are made."

"And when shall I see her?"

"Not for some time yet," answered the king, and the tears came into his eyes.

Irene did not remember her mother and did not know why her father looked so, and why the tears came in his eyes. But she put her arms around his neck and kissed him, and asked no more questions.

The king was much disturbed on hearing the report of the gentlemen-at-arms concerning the creatures they had seen, and, I presume, would have taken Irene with him that very day, except for the presence of the ring on her finger, and what it told him. About an hour before he left, Irene saw him go up the old stairs. He did not come down again till they were just ready to start; and she thought that he had been up to see the old lady.

When he went away, he left another six gentlemen behind him, so there might be six of them always on guard.

10   Goblin Counsels

In the caverns beneath the mountain, Curdie was as watchful as ever, but was almost getting tired of his ill success. Every other night or so he followed the goblins about as they went on digging and boring, and getting as near them as he could, watched them from behind stones and rocks. He always kept hold of the end of his string, while his pickax, left just outside the hole by which he passed from the mine into the goblins' country, continued to serve as an anchor and hold fast the other end.

One night, after dodging about and listening till he was nearly falling asleep with weariness, he began to roll up his ball, for he had resolved to go home to bed. It was not long, however, before he began to feel bewildered. One after another he passed goblin caves, occupied by goblin families, and at length was sure there were many more than he had passed as he came. Could his string have led him wrong? He still followed winding it, and still it led him into more thickly populated quarters, until he became quite uneasy; for although he was not afraid of the cobs, he was afraid of not finding his way out. But what could he do? It was of no use to sit down and wait for morning—the morning made no difference here. It was always dark; and if his string failed him he was helpless. He might even arrive within a yard of the mine and never know it.

Seeing he could do nothing better, he decided to find where the end of his string was and how it had come to play him such a trick. He knew by the size of the ball that he was getting pretty near the last of it, when he began to feel a tugging and pulling. What could it mean? Turning a sharp corner, he thought he heard strange sounds. These grew, as he went on, to a scuffling and growling and squeaking. The noise increased, until, turning a second sharp corner, he found himself in the midst of a wallowing mass, which he knew must be a knot of the cobs' creatures.

Before he could get to his feet, he had caught some great scratches on his face and several severe bites on his legs and arms. But as he scrambled to get up, his hand fell upon his pickax, and before the horrid beasts could do him any serious harm, he was swinging about with it right and left in the dark. Their hideous cries, the scampering, and retreating howls gave him the satisfaction of knowing that he had routed them.

He stood for a little, weighing his battle-ax in his hand as if it had been the most precious lump of metal, then untied the end of the string from it, put the ball in his pocket, and still stood thinking. It was clear that the cobs' creatures had found his ax, had between them carried it off, and had so led him he knew not where. But for all his thinking he could not tell what he ought to do, until he suddenly became aware of a glimmer of light in the distance. Without a moment's hesitation he set out for it, as fast as the unknown and rugged way would permit. He came at length to a small chamber in which an opening, high in the wall, revealed a glow beyond. To this opening he managed to scramble up, and then he saw a strange sight.

Below sat a little group of goblins around a fire, the smoke of which vanished in the darkness far aloft. The sides of the cave were full of shining minerals like those of the palace hall; and the company was evidently of a superior order, for everyone wore stones about head, or arms, or waist, shining dull, gorgeous colors in the light of the fire. Nor had Curdie looked long before he recognized the king himself, and found that he had made his way into the inner apartment of the royal family!

He crept through the hole as softly as he could, scrambled a good way down the wall towards them without attracting attention, and then sat down and listened. The king, evidently the queen, and probably the crown prince and the prime minister were talking together. He was sure of the queen by her shoes, for as she warmed her feet at the fire, he saw them quite plainly.

"That will be fun!" said the one he took for the crown prince.

It was the first whole sentence he heard.

"I don't see why you should think the marriage such a grand affair!" said his stepmother, tossing her head backward.

"You must remember, my spouse," interposed His Majesty, as if making excuses for his son, "he has got the same blood in him. His mother—"

"Don't talk to me of his mother! You positively encourage his unnatural fancies. Whatever belongs to *that* mother ought to be cut out of him. If you expect *me* to approve of such coarse tastes, you will find yourself mistaken. *I* don't wear shoes for nothing."

"You must acknowledge, however," the king said, with a little groan, "that this is no whim of Harelip's, but a matter of state policy. You are well aware that his gratification comes purely from the pleasure of sacrificing himself to the public good. Does it not, Harelip?"

"Yes, father. Of course it does. Only it *will* be nice to make her cry. I'll have the skin taken off between her toes, and tie them up till they grow together. Then her feet will be like other people's, and there will be no occasion for her to wear shoes."

"Do you mean to insinuate *I've* got toes, you unnatural wretch?" cried the queen, and she moved angrily towards Harelip. The councillor, however, who was betwixt them, leaned forward so as to prevent her touching him.

"Your Royal Highness," he said to the prince, "possibly requires to be reminded that you have got three toes yourself—one on one foot, two on the other."

"Ha! ha! ha!" shouted the queen triumphantly.

The councillor, encouraged by this mark of favor, went on. "It seems to me, Your Royal Highness, it would greatly endear you to your future people if you were to command upon yourself the comparatively slight operation which, in a more extended form, you so wisely meditate with regard to your future princess."

"Ha! ha! ha!" laughed the queen louder than before, and the king and the minister joined in the laugh. Harelip growled, and for a few moments the others continued to express their enjoyment of his discomfort.

The queen was the only one Curdie could see with any distinctness. She sat sideways to him, and the light of the fire shone full upon her face. He could not consider her handsome. Her nose was certainly broad, and her eyes, instead of being horizontal, were set up like two perpendicular eggs, one on the broad, the other on the small end. Her mouth was no bigger than a small buttonhole until she laughed, when it stretched from ear to ear—only to be sure, her ears were very nearly in the middle of her cheeks.

69

Anxious to hear everything they might say, Curdie ventured to slide down a smooth part of the rock just under him to a projection below. But whether he was not careful enough, or the projection gave way, down he came with a rush on the floor of the cavern, bringing with him a great, rumbling shower of stones.

The goblins jumped from their seats in anger. But when they saw Curdie with his pick in his hand their rage was mingled with fear, for they took him for the first of an invasion of miners. The king drew himself up to his full height of four feet, spread himself to his full breadth of three and a half, for he was the handsomest and squarest of all the goblins, and strutting up to Curdie, planted himself with outspread feet before him, and said with dignity, "Pray what right have you in my palace?"

"The right of necessity, Your Majesty," answered Curdie. "I lost my way and did not know where I was wandering to."

"How did you get in?"

"By a hole in the mountain."

"But you are a miner! Look at your pickax!"

Curdie did look at it, answering, "I came upon it lying on the ground a little way from here. I tumbled over some wild beasts who were playing with it. Look, Your Majesty." And Curdie showed him how he was scratched and bitten.

The king was pleased to find him behave more politely than he had expected from what his people had told him concerning the miners. But he attributed it to the power of his own presence, and he did not feel friendly to the intruder.

"You will oblige me by walking out of my dominions at once."

"With pleasure, if Your Majesty will give me a guide," said Curdie.

"I will give you a thousand," said the king. He uttered a strange shout, half halloo, half roar, and in rushed goblins till the cave was swarming. He said something to the first of them, which Curdie could not hear, and it was passed from one to another till in a moment the farthest in the crowd had evidently heard and understood it. They began to gather about Curdie in a way he did not relish, and he retreated towards the wall.

"Stand back," said Curdie, grasping his pickax tighter by his knee.

They only grinned and pressed closer. Curdie began to make up a rhyme.

> "Ten, twenty, thirty—
> You're all so very dirty!
> Twenty, thirty, forty—
> You're all so thick and snorty!

"Thirty, forty, fifty—
You're all so puff-and-snifty!
Forty, fifty, sixty—
Beast and man so mixty!

"Fifty, sixty, seventy—
Mixty, maxty, leaventy!
Sixty, seventy, eighty—
All your cheeks so slaty!

"Seventy, eighty, ninety,
All your hands so flinty!
Eighty, ninety, hundred,
Altogether dundred!"

The goblins fell back a little when he began, and made horrible grimaces all through the rhyme, as if eating something so disagreeable that it set their teeth on edge and gave them the creeps. Whether it was that most of the rhyming words were not words at all, or whether it was that the presence of the king and queen gave them courage, I cannot tell. But the moment the rhyme was over they crowded on him again, and out shot a hundred long arms, with a multitude of thick, nailless fingers at the ends of them, to lay hold upon him.

Then Curdie heaved up his ax. But being as gentle as he was courageous, and not wishing to kill any of them, he turned the end which was square and blunt like a hammer, and with that came down a great blow on the head of the goblin nearest him.

The goblin only gave a horrible cry, and sprung at Curdie's throat. Curdie, however, drew back in time, and just at that critical moment remembered the vulnerable part of the goblin body. He made a sudden rush at the king and stamped with all his might on His Majesty's feet. The king gave a most unkingly howl and almost fell into the fire. Curdie then rushed into the crowd, stamping right and left. The goblins drew back, howling on every side as he approached, but they were so crowded that few of those he attacked could escape his tread.

They were tumbling over each other in heaps in their eagerness to rush from the cave, when a new assailant suddenly faced Curdie: the queen. With flaming eyes and expanded nostrils, her hair standing half up from her head, she rushed at him. She trusted in her shoes; for they were of granite, hollowed like French sabots. Curdie would have endured much rather than hurt a woman, even if she was a goblin, but here was an affair of life and death. Forgetting her shoes, he made a great stamp on one of her feet. But she instantly returned the stamp, causing him frightful pain, and almost disabling him. His only chance would have been to attack the granite shoes with his pickax, but before he could think of that she had caught him up in her arms and was rushing with him across the cave.

She dashed him into a hole in the wall, with a force that almost stunned him. But although he could not move, he was not too far gone to hear her great cry, and the rush of multitudes of soft feet, followed by the sounds of something heaved up against the rock. After that came a multitudinous patter of stones falling near him. The last had not ceased when he grew very faint, for his head had been badly cut, and at last he fell unconscious.

When he came to himself there was perfect silence about him, and utter darkness, but for the merest glimmer in one tiny spot. He crawled to it, and found that the goblins had heaved a slab against the mouth of the hole, past the edge of which a poor little gleam found its way from the fire. He could not move it a hairbreadth, for they had piled a great heap of stones against it. He crawled back to where he had been lying, in the faint hope of finding his pickax. But after a vain search he was at last compelled to acknowledge himself in an evil plight. He sat down and tried to think, but soon fell fast asleep.

He must have slept a long time, for when he awoke he felt wonderfully restored—indeed almost well—and very hungry. There were voices in the outer cave.

Once more, it was night; for the goblins slept during the day and went about their affairs during the night. Curdie listened, and soon found that they were talking of himself.

"How long will it take?" asked Harelip.

"Not many days, I should think," answered the king. "They are poor feeble creatures, those sun people, and want to be always eating. We can go a week at a time without food, and be all the better for it. But I've been told they eat two or three times every day! Can you believe it?"

"If I may be allowed a word," interposed the queen, "—and I think I ought to have some voice in the matter—"

"The wretch is entirely at your disposal, my spouse," interrupted the king. "He is your property. You caught him yourself. We should never have done it."

The queen laughed. She seemed in far better humor than the night before. "I

was about to say that it does seem a pity to waste so much fresh meat. By the time he is starved there will hardly be a picking upon his bones."

The king gave a great laugh. "Well, my spouse, you may have him when you like," he said. "I don't fancy him, for my part. I am pretty sure he is tough eating."

"For me to eat him would be to honor instead of punish his insolence." returned the queen. "But why should our poor creatures be deprived of so much nourishment? Our little dogs and cats and pigs and small bears would enjoy him very much."

"You are the best of housekeepers, my lovely queen!" said her husband. "Let it be so, by all means. Let us have our people in, and get him out and kill him at once. He deserves it. The mischief he might have brought upon us, now that he had penetrated so far as our most secret citadel, is incalculable. Or rather let us tie him hand and foot, and have the pleasure of seeing him torn to pieces by full torchlight in the great hall."

"Better and better!" cried the queen and the prince together, both of them clapping their hands. And the prince made a smacking noise with his lips, as if he intended to join in the feast.

"But," added the queen, "he is so troublesome. For, poor creatures as they are, there is something about those sun people that is very troublesome. I cannot imagine how it is that with such superior strength and skill and understanding as ours, we permit them to exist at all. Why do we not destroy them entirely, and use their cattle and grazing lands at our pleasure? Of course we don't want to live in their horrid country! But we might use it as a sort of outhouse, and even keep their great cows and other creatures, and then we should have a few more luxuries, such as cream and cheese."

"It is worth thinking of," said the king, "and you have a positive genius for conquest. But still, as you say, there is something very troublesome about them. It would be better, as I understand you to suggest, that we should starve him for a day or two first, so that he may be a little less frisky when we take him out."

> "Once there was a goblin
> Living in a hole;
> Busy he was cobblin'
> A shoe without a sole.
>
> "By came a birdie;
> 'Goblin, what do you do?'

74

'Cobble at a sturdy
Upper leather shoe.'

" 'What's the good o' that, sir?'
Said the little bird.
" 'Why it's very pat, sir—
Plain without a word.

" 'Where 'tis all a hole, sir,
Never can be holes:
Why should their shoes have soles, sir,
When they've got no souls?' "

"What's that horrible noise?" cried the queen, shuddering from pot-metal head to granite shoes.

"I declare," said the king with solemn indignation, "it's the sun creature in the hole!"

"Stop that disgusting noise!" cried the crown prince valiantly, getting up and standing in front of the heap of stones, with his face towards Curdie's prison. "Do now, or I'll break your head."

"Break away," shouted Curdie, and began singing again:

"Once there was a goblin,
Living in a hole—"

"I really can*not* bear it," said the queen. "If I could only get at his horrid toes with my slippers—again!"

"I think we had better go to bed," said the king.

Curdie began singing again:

"Go to bed,
Goblin, do.
Help the queen
Take off her shoe.

"If you do,
It will disclose
A horrid set
Of sprouting toes."

"What a lie!" roared the queen in a rage.

"By the way, that reminds me," said the king, "that for as long as we have

75

been married, I have never seen your feet, queen. I think you might take off your shoes when you go to bed! They positively hurt me sometimes."

"I will do as I like," retorted the queen sulkily.

"You ought to do as your own hubby wishes you," said the king.

"I will not," said the queen.

"Then I insist upon it," said the king.

Apparently His Majesty approached the queen for the purpose of following the advice given by Curdie, for the latter heard a scuffle, and then a great roar from the king.

"Will you be quiet, then?" said the queen wickedly.

"Yes, yes, queen. I only meant to coax you."

"Hands off!" cried the queen triumphantly. "I'm going to bed. You may come when you like. But as long as I am queen I will sleep in my shoes. It is my royal privilege. Harelip, go to bed."

"I'm going," said Harelip sleepily.

"So am I," said the king.

"Come along, then," said the queen, "and mind you are good, or I'll—"

"Oh, no, no, no!" screamed the king in the most supplicating of tones.

Curdie heard only a muttered reply in the distance; and then the cave was quite still.

They had left the fire burning, and the light came through brighter than before. Curdie thought it was time to try again if anything could be done. But he found he could not get even a finger through the chink between the slab and the rock. He gave a great rush with his shoulder against the slab, but it yielded no more than if it had been part of the rock. All he could do was to sit down and think again.

By and by he came to the resolution to pretend to be dying, in the hope they might take him out before his strength was too much exhausted to let him have a chance. Then if he could but find his ax again, he would have no fear of them. And if it were not for the queen's horrid shoes, he would have no fear at all.

Meantime, until they should come again at night, there was nothing for him to do but forge new rhymes, for they were now his only weapons.

11 Irene's Thread

That same morning early, the princess woke in a terrible fright. There was a hideous noise in her room—of creatures snarling and hissing and racketing about as if they were fighting. The moment she came to herself, she remembered what her grandmother told her to do when she was frightened. She immediately took off her ring and put it under her pillow. As she did so she fancied she felt a finger and thumb take it gently from under her palm.

It must be my grandmother! she said to herself, and the thought gave her such courage that she stopped to put on her dainty little slippers before running from the room. While doing this she caught sight of a long cloak of sky blue, thrown over the back of a chair by the bedside. She had never seen it before, but it was evidently waiting for her. She put it on, and then, feeling with the forefinger of her right hand, soon found her grandmother's thread, which she proceeded at once to follow, expecting it would lead her straight up the old stair.

When she reached the door, she found it went down and ran along the floor, so that she had almost to crawl in order to keep a hold of it. Then, to her surprise, and somewhat to her dismay, she found that instead of leading her towards the stair it turned in quite the opposite direction. It led her through

77

certain narrow passages towards the kitchen, turning aside ere she reached it and guiding her to a door that communicated with a small backyard. Across the yard the thread still ran along the ground, until it brought her to a door in the wall, which opened up on the mountainside. When she had passed through the doorway, the thread rose to about half her height, and she could hold it with ease as she walked. It led her straight up the mountain.

It was a clear, warm morning. The wind blew deliciously over the mountainside. Here and there Irene saw a late primrose, but she did not stop to call upon any of them. The sky was mottled with small clouds. The sun was not yet up, but some of their fluffy edges had caught his light, and hung out orange- and gold-colored fringes upon the air.

How lovely that bit of gossamer is! thought the princess, looking at a long, undulating line that shone at some distance from her up the hill. It was not the time for gossamers though, and Irene soon discovered that it was her own thread she saw shining on before her in the light of the morning. She knew not where it was leading her. But she had never in her life been out before sunrise, and everything was so fresh and cool and lively that she felt too happy to be afraid of anything.

After a good distance, the thread turned to the left, and down the path upon which she and Lootie had met Curdie. But she never thought of that, for now in the morning light, with its far outlook over the country, no path could have been more open and airy and cheerful.

Down and down the path went, then up, and then down and then up again, getting more rugged as it went. And still along the path went the silvery thread, and still along the thread went Irene's little forefinger.

By and by she came to a little stream that jabbered and prattled down the hill. Up the side of the stream went both path and thread. The path grew rougher and steeper, and the mountain grew wilder, till Irene began to think she was going a very long way from home. When she turned to look back, she saw that the level country had vanished and the rough, bare mountain had closed in about her. But still on went the thread, and on went the princess.

Everything around her was getting brighter and brighter as the sun came nearer; till at length his first rays all at once alighted on the top of a rock before her, like some golden creature fresh from the sky. Then she saw that the little stream ran out of a hole in that rock; the path did not go past the rock, and the thread was leading her straight up to it. A shudder ran through her from head to foot when she found that the thread was actually taking her into the hole. The stream ran out of the mountain babbling joyously, but she had to go in.

78

She did not hesitate. Right into the hole she went, which was high enough to let her walk without stooping. For a little way there was a brown glimmer. But at the first turn it all but ceased, and before she had gone many paces she was in total darkness. Then she began to be frightened indeed. Every moment she kept feeling the thread backwards and forwards. As she went farther and farther into the darkness of the great, hollow mountain, she kept thinking more and more about her grandmother, and all that she had said to her, and how kind she had been, and how beautiful she was, and all about her lovely room, and the fire of roses, and the great lamp that sent its light through stone walls.

She became more and more sure that the thread could not have gone there itself; her grandmother must have sent it. But it tried her dreadfully when the path went down very steep, and especially when she came to places where she had to go down rough stairs, and even sometimes a ladder. Through one narrow passage after another, over lumps of rock and sand and clay, the thread guided her, until she came to a small hole through which she had to creep. Sometimes she heard the noise of water, a dull gurgling inside the rock. By and by she heard the sounds of blows, which came nearer and nearer; but again they grew duller, and almost died away. In a hundred directions she turned, obedient to the guiding thread.

At last she spied a dull red shine, and came right into a cavern, where glowed the red embers of a fire. Here the thread began to rise. It rose as high as her head and higher still. What should she do if she lost her hold? She was pulling it down! She might break it! She could see it far up, glowing as red as her fire opal in the light of the embers.

But presently she came to a huge heap of stones, piled in a slope against the wall of the cavern. On these she climbed, and soon recovered the level of the thread—only to find, the next moment, that it vanished through the heap of stones, and left her standing on it, with her face to the solid rock. For one terrible moment she felt as if her grandmother had forsaken her. The thread had gone where she could no longer follow it, had brought her into a horrible cavern, and left her there.

She threw herself upon the heap, and began to cry. It was well she did not know that creatures, one of them with stone shoes on her feet, were lying in the next cave.

At length the thought struck her that she could at least follow the thread backwards, and thus get out of the mountain and home. She rose at once, and found the thread. But the instant she tried to feel it backwards, it vanished from her touch. Forwards, it led her hand up to the heap of stones; backwards it went nowhere. Neither could she see it as she had before in the light of the fire. She burst into a wailing cry, and again threw herself down on the stones.

As the princess lay and sobbed she kept feeling the thread mechanically, following it with her finger many times up to the stones in which it disappeared. By and by she began, still mechanically, to poke her finger in between the stones as far as she could. All at once it came into her head that she might remove some of the stones and see where the thread went next.

Almost laughing at herself for never having thought of this before, she jumped to her feet. Her fear vanished; once more she was certain her grandmother's thread could not have brought her there just to leave her. She began to throw away the stones from the top as fast as she could, sometimes two or three at a handful, sometimes taking both hands to lift one. After clearing them away a little, she found that the thread turned and went straight downwards. She began to be afraid that to clear the thread she must remove the whole huge gathering of stones. She was dismayed at the very idea, but, losing no time, set to work with a will. With aching back and bleeding fingers and hands, she worked on, sustained by the pleasure of seeing the heap slowly diminish. As often as she uncovered a turn of the thread, it tightened up, instead of lying loose upon the stones. This made her sure that her grandmother was at the other end of it somewhere.

She had got about halfway down when she nearly fell with fright. Close to her ears, a voice broke out singing:

> "Jabber, bother, smash!
> You'll have it all in a crash.
> Jabber, smash, bother!
> You'll have the worst of the pother.
> Smash, bother, jabber!—"

Here Curdie stopped, either because he could not find a rhyme to *jabber*, or because he remembered that his plan was to make the goblins think he was getting weak. But he had uttered enough to let Irene know who he was.

"It's Curdie!" she cried joyfully.

"Hush! hush!" came Curdie's voice from somewhere. "Speak softly."

"Why, you were singing loud!"

"Yes. But they know I am here, and they don't know you are. Who are you?"

"I'm Irene," answered the princess. "I know who you are quite well. You're Curdie."

"Why, however did you come here, Irene?"

"My great-great-grandmother sent me, and I think I've found out why. You can't get out, I suppose?"

"No, I can't. What are you doing?"

"Clearing away a huge heap of stones."

"There's a princess!" exclaimed Curdie, in a tone of delight, but still speaking in little more than a whisper. "I can't think how you got here, though."

"My grandmother sent me after her thread."

"I don't know what you mean," said Curdie. "But you can tell me all about it when we get out. There's no time to lose now."

Irene went to work, as fresh as when she began. "There's such a lot of stones! It will take me a long time to get them all away."

"How far on have you gotten?"

"I've gotten about the half away, but the other half is ever so much bigger."

"I don't think you will have to move the lower half. Do you see a slab laid up against the wall?"

Irene looked, and felt about with her hands, and soon perceived the outlines of the slab. "Yes," she answered, "I do."

"Then, when you have cleared the slab about halfway down, or a little more, I shall be able to push it over."

"I must follow my thread," returned Irene, "whatever I do."

"What do you mean?" exclaimed Curdie.

"You will see when you get out," answered the princess, and went on harder than ever.

But she was soon satisfied that what Curdie wanted done and what the thread wanted done were one and the same thing. As soon as she realized this, she said in a right joyous whisper, "Now, Curdie! I think if you were to give a great push, the slab would tumble over."

"Stand quite clear of it, then," said Curdie, "and let me know when you are ready."

Irene got off the heap, and stood on one side of it. "Now, Curdie!" she cried.

Curdie gave a great rush with his shoulder against it. Out tumbled the slab on the heap, and out crept Curdie over the top of it.

"You've saved my life, Irene!" he whispered.

"Oh, Curdie! I'm so glad! Let's get out of this horrid place as fast as we can."

"That's easier said than done."

"Oh, no! It's quite easy. We have only to follow my thread. I am sure that it's going to take us out now."

She had already begun to follow it over the fallen slab into the hole, while

Curdie was searching the floor of the cavern for his pickax.

"Here it is!" he cried. "No, it is not!" he added, in a disappointed tone. "What can it be, then? I declare it's a torch. That is jolly! It's better almost than my pickax. Much better if it weren't for those stone shoes!" he went on, as he lighted the torch by blowing on the last embers of the expiring fire.

When he looked up, with the lighted torch casting a glare into the great darkness of the huge cavern, he caught sight of Irene disappearing in the hole out of which he had himself just come.

"Where are you going there?" he cried. "That's not the way out. That's where I couldn't get out."

"I know that," whispered Irene. "But this is the way my thread goes, and I must follow it."

What nonsense the child talks! said Curdie to himself. *I must follow her, though, and see that she comes to no harm. She will soon find she can't get out that way, and then she will come with me.*

So he crept over the slab once more into the hole with his torch in his hand. But when he looked about in it, he could see her nowhere. And now he discovered that although the hole was narrow, it was much longer than he had supposed. For in one direction the roof came down very low, and the hole went off in a narrow passage, of which he could not see the end. The princess must have crept in there.

He got on his knees and one hand, holding the torch with the other, and crept after her. The hole twisted about, in some parts so low that he could hardly get through, in others so high that he could not see the roof, but everywhere it was narrow—far too narrow for a goblin to get through, and so I presume they never thought that Curdie might. He was beginning to feel very uncomfortable lest something should have befallen the princess, when he heard her voice almost close to his ear, whispering, "Aren't you coming, Curdie?"

When he turned the next corner, she stood waiting for him. "I knew you couldn't go wrong in that narrow hole, but now you must keep by me, for here is a great wide place."

"I can't understand it," said Curdie, half to himself, half to Irene.

"Never mind," she returned. "Wait till we get out."

Curdie, utterly astonished that she had already gotten so far, and by a path he had known nothing of, thought it better to let her do as she pleased. He followed her a few steps, and came out in another great cavern, across which Irene walked in a straight line, as confidently as if she knew every step of the way. Curdie went on after her, flashing his torch about, and trying to see something of what lay around them.

Suddenly he started back a pace as the light fell upon something close by which Irene was passing. It was a platform of rock raised a few feet from the floor and covered with sheepskins, upon which lay two horrible figures asleep, at once recognized by Curdie as the king and queen of the goblins. He lowered his torch instantly lest the light should awaken them. As he did so it flashed upon his pickax, lying by the side of the queen.

"Stop one moment," he whispered. "Hold my torch, and don't let the light on their faces."

Irene shuddered when she saw the frightful creatures, but she did as he requested, and turning her back, held the torch low in front of her. Curdie drew his pickax carefully away, and as he did so spied one of the queen's feet, projecting from under the skins. The great, clumsy, granite shoe, exposed thus to his hand, was a temptation not to be resisted. He laid hold of it, and, with cautious efforts, drew it off.

The moment he succeeded, he saw to his astonishment that what he had sung in ignorance, to annoy the queen, was actually true: she had six horrible toes. Overjoyed at his success, and seeing by the huge bump in the sheepskins where the other foot was, he proceeded to lift them gently, for, if he could only succeed in carrying away the other shoe as well, he would be no more afraid of the goblins than of so many flies. But as he pulled on the second shoe the queen gave a growl and sat up in bed. The same instant the king awoke also and sat up beside her.

"Run, Irene!" cried Curdie, for though he was not now in the least afraid for himself, he was for the princess.

Irene looked once around, saw the fearful creatures awake, and like the wise princess she was, dashed the torch on the ground and extinguished it, crying out: "Here, Curdie, take my hand."

He darted to her side, forgetting neither the queen's shoe nor his pickax, and caught hold of her hand as she sped fearlessly where her thread guided her. They heard the queen give a great bellow; but they had a good start, for it would be some time before they could get torches lighted to pursue them. Just as they thought they saw a gleam behind them, the thread brought them to a very narrow opening, through which Irene crept easily, and Curdie with difficulty.

"Now," said Curdie, "I think we shall be safe."

"Of course," returned Irene. "My grandmother is taking care of us."

"That's all nonsense. I don't know what you mean."

"Then if you don't know what I mean, what right have you to call it nonsense?" asked the princess, a little offended.

"I beg your pardon, Irene. I did not mean to vex you."

"Of course not," returned the princess. "But why do you think we shall be safe?"

"Because the king and queen are far too stout to get through that hole."

"There might be ways around."

"To be sure there might; we are not out of it yet," acknowledged Curdie.

"But what do you mean by the king and queen?" asked the princess. "I should never call such creatures as those a king and a queen."

"Their own people do, though."

The princess asked more questions, and Curdie, as they walked leisurely along, gave her a full account, not only of the character and habits of the goblins, so far as he knew them, but of his own adventures, beginning with the very night after he had met her and Lootie upon the mountain. When he had finished, he begged Irene to tell him how it was that she had come to his rescue.

So Irene, too, had to tell a long story, which she did in rather a roundabout manner, interrupted by many questions concerning things she had not explained. But as Curdie did not believe more than half of her tale, it left everything as unaccountable to him as before.

"But however did Lootie come to let you go into the mountains alone?"

"Lootie knows nothing about it. I left her fast asleep, at least I think so. I hope my grandmother won't let her get into trouble, for it wasn't her fault at all."

"But how did you find your way to me?"

"I told you already," answered Irene, "by keeping my finger upon my grandmother's thread, as I am doing now."

"You don't mean you've got the thread there?"

"Of course I do. I have told you so ten times already. I have hardly—except when I was removing the stones—taken my finger off it. There!" she added, guiding Curdie's hand to the thread, "you feel it yourself, don't you?"

"I feel nothing at all," replied Curdie.

"Then what can be the matter with your finger? I feel it perfectly. To be sure it is very thin, and in the sunlight looks just like the thread of a spider, but I can't think why you shouldn't feel it as well as I do."

Curdie was too polite to say he did not believe there was any thread there at all. What he did say was: "Well, I can make nothing of it."

"I can, though, and you must be glad of that, for it will do for both of us," returned Irene confidently. And now the thread went downwards, and led Irene's hand to a hole in the floor of the cavern, whence came a sound of running water, which they had been hearing for some time.

"It goes into the ground now, Curdie," she said, stopping.

He had been listening to another sound, which his practiced ear had caught long ago—and had been growing louder. It was the noise the goblin miners made at their work, and they seemed to be at no great distance now. Irene heard it the moment she stopped.

"What is that noise?" she asked.

"It is the goblins digging and burrowing."

"And you don't know what they do it for?"

"No, I haven't the least idea. Would you like to see them?" he asked, wishing to have another try after their secret.

"If my thread took me there, I shouldn't much mind. But my thread leads me down into the hole, and we had better go at once."

"Very well. Shall I go in first?"

"No. You can't feel the thread," she answered, stepping down through a narrow break in the floor of the cavern. "Oh!" she cried, "I am in the water. It is running strong; but it is not deep, and there is just room to walk. Make haste, Curdie."

He tried, but the hole was too small for him to get in. "Go on a little bit," he said, shouldering his pickax.

In a few moments he had cleared a larger opening and followed her. They went on, down and down with the running water, Curdie getting more and more afraid it was leading them to some terrible gulf in the heart of the mountain. In one or two places he had to break away the rock to make room before even Irene could get through—at least without hurting herself. But at length they spied a glimmer of light, and in a minute more they were almost blinded by the full sunlight, into which they emerged. It was some little time before the princess could see well enough to discover that they stood in her own garden, close by the seat on which she and her king-papa had sat that other afternoon. They had come out by the channel of the little stream. She danced and clapped hands with delight.

"Now, Curdie!" she cried, "won't you believe what I told you about my grandmother and her thread?"

For she had felt all the time that Curdie was not believing what she told him. "There! Don't you see it shining on before us?" she added.

"I don't see anything," persisted Curdie.

"Then you must believe without seeing," said the princess. "For you can't deny it has brought us out of the mountain."

"I can't deny we are out of the mountain, and I should be very ungrateful indeed to deny that you had brought me out of it."

"I couldn't have done it but for the thread," persisted Irene.

"That's the part I don't understand."

"Well, come along, and Lootie will get you something to eat. I am sure you must want it very much."

"Indeed I do. But my father and mother will be so anxious about me, I must make haste—first up the mountain to tell my mother and then down into the mine again to let my father know."

"Very well, Curdie. But you can't get out without coming this way, and I will take you through the house, for that is nearest."

They met no one by the way, for, indeed, as before, the people were here and there and everywhere searching for the princess. When they got inside Irene found that the thread, as she had half expected, went up the old staircase, and a new thought struck her.

She turned to Curdie and said: "My grandmother wants me. Do come up with me and see her. Then you will know that I have been telling you the truth. Do come—to please me, Curdie. I can't bear you should think what I say is not true."

"I never doubted you believed what you said," returned Curdie. "I only thought you had some fancy in your head that was not correct."

"But do come, dear Curdie."

The little miner could not withstand this appeal, and though he felt shy in what seemed to him a huge, grand house, he yielded, and followed her up the stair.

12　The Old Lady and Curdie

Up the stair they went, and the next and the next, and through the long rows of empty rooms, and up the little tower stair, Irene growing happier and happier as she ascended. There was no answer when she knocked at the door of the workroom, nor could she hear any sound of the spinning wheel. Once more her heart sank within her, but only for one moment, as she turned and knocked at the other door.

"Come in," answered the sweet voice of her grandmother, and Irene opened the door and entered, followed by Curdie.

"You darling!" cried the lady, who was seated by a fire of red roses mingled with white. "I've been waiting for you, and indeed getting a little anxious about you, and beginning to think whether I had not better go and fetch you myself."

As she spoke she took the little princess in her arms and placed her upon her lap. She was dressed in white now, looking if possible more lovely than ever.

"I've brought Curdie, grandmother. He wouldn't believe what I told him and so I've brought him."

"Yes, I see him. He is a good boy, Curdie, and a brave boy. Aren't you glad you've got him out?"

"Yes, grandmother. But it wasn't very good of him not to believe me when I was telling him the truth."

"People must believe what they can, and those who believe more must not be hard upon those who believe less. I doubt if you would have believed it all yourself if you hadn't seen some of it."

"Ah! yes, grandmother, I daresay you are right. But he'll believe now."

"I don't know that," replied her grandmother.

"Won't you, Curdie?" said Irene, looking round at him as she asked the question.

He was standing in the middle of the floor, staring, and looking strangely bewildered. This she thought came of his astonishment at the beauty of the lady.

"Make a bow to my grandmother, Curdie," she said.

"I don't see any grandmother," answered Curdie rather gruffly.

"Don't see my grandmother, when I'm sitting in her lap?" exclaimed the princess.

"No, I don't," reiterated Curdie, in an offended tone.

"Don't you see the lovely fire of roses—white ones amongst them this time?" asked Irene, almost as bewildered as he.

"No, I don't," answered Curdie, almost sulkily.

"Nor the blue bed? Nor the rose-colored counterpane? Nor the beautiful light, like the moon, hanging from the roof?"

"You're making game of me, Your Royal Highness. After what we have come through together this day, I don't think it is kind of you," said Curdie, feeling very much hurt.

"Then what do you see?" asked Irene, who perceived at once that for her not to believe him was at least as bad as for him not to believe her.

"I see a big, bare, garret room—like the one in mother's cottage, only big enough to take the cottage itself in and leave a good margin all around."

"And what more do you see?"

"I see a tub, and a heap of musty straw, and a withered apple, and a ray of sunlight coming through a hole in the middle of the roof and shining on your head, making all the place look a curious dusky brown. I think you had better drop it, princess, and go down to the nursery, like a good girl."

"But don't you hear my grandmother talking to me?" asked Irene, almost crying.

"No. I hear the cooing of a lot of pigeons. If you won't come down, I will go without you. I think that will be better, anyhow, for I'm sure nobody who met us would believe a word we said to them. They would think we made it all up. I don't expect anybody but my own father and mother to believe me. They know I wouldn't tell a story."

"And yet you won't believe me, Curdie?" pleaded the princess, now fairly crying with vexation and sorrow.

"No. I can't, and I can't help it," said Curdie, turning to leave the room.

"What shall I do, grandmother?" sobbed the princess, turning her face to the lady's bosom and shaking with suppressed sobs.

"You must give him time," said her grandmother. "And you must be content not to be believed for a while. It is very hard to bear; but I have had to bear it, and shall have to bear it many a time yet. I will take care of what Curdie thinks of you in the end. You must let him go now."

"You're not coming, are you?" asked Curdie.

"No, Curdie, my grandmother says I must let you go. Turn to the right when you get to the bottom of all the stairs, and that will take you to the hall where the great door is."

"Oh! I don't doubt I can find my way without you, princess, or your old grannie's thread either." Curdie said this as he opened the door, and, without another word, went down the stair. Irene listened with dismay to his departing footsteps.

"What does it all mean, grandmother?" she sobbed, and burst into fresh tears.

"It means, my love, that I did not mean to show myself. Curdie is not yet able to believe some things. Seeing is not believing—it is only seeing. You remember I told you that if Lootie were to see me, she would rub her eyes, forget the half she saw, and call the other half nonsense."

"Yes, but I should have thought Curdie—"

"You are right. Curdie is much farther on than Lootie, and you will see what will come of it. But in the meantime you must be content to be misunderstood for a while. We are all very anxious to be understood, and it is very hard not to be. But there is one thing much more important."

"What is that, grandmother?"

"To understand other people."

"Yes, grandmother. I must be fair; for if I'm not fair to other people, I'm not worth being understood myself. So as Curdie can't help it, I will not be vexed with him, but just wait."

"There's my own dear child," said her grandmother, and pressed her close to her bosom.

"There is one thing that puzzles me," said the princess. "How are you to get the thread out of the mountain again? Surely you won't have to make another for me? That would be such a trouble!"

The lady set her down and rose and went to the fire. Putting in her hand, she drew it out again and held up the shining ball between her finger and thumb.

"I've got it now, you see," she said, coming back to the princess, "all ready for you when you want it." Going to her cabinet, she laid it in the same drawer as before.

"And here is your ring," she added, taking it from the little finger of her left hand and putting it on the forefinger of Irene's right hand.

"Oh, thank you, grandmother! I feel so safe now!"

"You are very tired, my child," the lady went on. "Your hands are hurt with the stones, and I have counted nine bruises on you. Just look what you are like."

And she held up a little mirror, which she had brought from the cabinet. The princess burst into a merry laugh at the sight. She was so draggled with the stream, and dirty with creeping through narrow places, that if she had seen the reflection without knowing it was a reflection, she would have taken herself for some gypsy child whose face was washed and hair combed about once in a month.

The lady laughed, too, and lifting her again upon her knee, took off her cloak and nightgown. Then she carried her to a large silver bath. As Irene looked into it, she saw no bottom, but the stars shining miles away, as it seemed, in a great blue gulf. Her hands closed involuntarily on the beautiful arms that held her.

"Do not be afraid, my child."

"No, grandmother," answered the princess, with a little gasp; and the next instant she sank in the clear, cool water.

When she opened her eyes, she saw nothing but a strange lovely blue over and beneath and all about her. The lady and the beautiful room had vanished from her sight, and she seemed utterly alone. But instead of being afraid, she felt more than happy—perfectly blissful. And from somewhere came the voice of the lady, singing a strange, sweet song, the sense of which she had only a feeling—no understanding. Nor could she remember a single line after it was gone. It vanished, like the poetry in a dream, as fast as it came. In after years, however, she would sometimes fancy that snatches of melody suddenly rising in her brain must be little phrases and fragments of the air of that song. And the song would make her happier, and abler to do her duty.

How long she lay in the water she did not know. But at last she felt the

beautiful hands lay hold of her, and through the gurgling water she was lifted out into the lovely room. The lady carried her to the fire, and sat down with her in her lap, and dried her tenderly with the softest towel. When the lady had done, she stooped to the fire, and drew from it her nightgown, as white as snow.

"How delicious!" exclaimed the princess. "It smells of all the roses in the world, I think."

When she stood up on the floor, she felt as if she had been made over again. Every bruise and all weariness were gone, and her hands were soft and whole as ever.

"Now I am going to put you to bed for a good sleep," said her grandmother.

"But what will Lootie be thinking? And what am I to say to her when she asks me where I have been?"

"Don't trouble yourself about it. You will find it all come right," said her grandmother, and laid her into the blue bed, under the rosy counterpane.

"There is just one thing more," said Irene. "I am a little anxious about Curdie. As I brought him into the house, I ought to have seen him safe on his way home."

"I took care of all that," answered the lady. "Nobody saw him, and he is now eating a good dinner in his mother's cottage far up in the mountain."

"Then I will go to sleep," said Irene, and she did.

13 Curdie and His Mother

Curdie went up the mountain neither whistling nor singing, for he was vexed with Irene for "taking him in," as he called it. And he was vexed with himself for having spoken to her so rudely.

His mother gave a cry of joy when she saw him, and at once set about getting him something to eat, asking him questions all the time, which he did not answer so cheerfully as usual. When his meal was ready, she left him to eat it, and hurried to the mine to let his father know he was safe. When she came back, she found him fast asleep upon her bed. Nor did he wake until his father came home in the evening.

"Now, Curdie," his mother said, as they sat at supper, "tell us the whole story from beginning to end, just as it all happened."

Curdie obeyed, and told everything to the point where they came out upon the lawn in the garden of the king's house.

"And what happened after that?" asked his mother. "You haven't told us all. You ought to be very happy at having got away from those demons, and instead of that I never saw you so gloomy. There must be something more. Besides, you do not speak of that lovely child as I should like to hear you. She saved your life at the risk of her own, and yet somehow you don't seem to think much of it."

"She talked such nonsense!" answered Curdie, "and told me a pack of things that weren't a bit true. I can't get over it."

"What were they?" asked his father. "Your mother may be able to throw some light upon them."

Then Curdie made a clean breast of it, and told them everything. They all sat silent for some time, pondering the strange tale.

At last Curdie's mother spoke. "You confess, my boy," she said, "there is something about the whole affair you do not understand?"

"Yes, of course, mother," he answered. "I cannot understand how a child knowing nothing about the mountain, or even that I was shut up in it, should come all that way alone, straight to where I was, then, after getting me out of the hole, lead me out of the mountain, too, where I should not have known a step of the way if it had been as light as in the open air."

"Then you have no right to say what she told you was not true. She did take you out, and she must have had something to guide her. Why not a thread as well as a rope, or anything else? There is something you cannot explain, and her explanation may be the right one."

"It's no explanation at all, mother. I can't believe it."

"That may be only because you do not understand it. If you did, you would probably find it was an explanation, and believe it thoroughly. I don't blame you for not being able to believe it, but I do blame you for fancying such a child would try to deceive you. Why should she? Depend upon it, she told you all she knew. Until you found a better way of accounting for it all, you might at least have been more sparing of your judgment."

"That is what something inside me has been saying all the time," said Curdie, hanging down his head. "But what do you make of the grandmother? That is what I can't get over. To take me up to an old garret, and try to persuade me against the sight of my own eyes that it was a beautiful room, with blue walls and silver stars, and no end of things in it, when there was nothing there but an old tub and a withered apple and a heap of straw and a sunbeam!"

"Didn't she speak as if she saw those other things herself, Curdie?"

"Yes. That's what bothers me. You would have thought she really believed that she saw every one of the things she talked about."

"Perhaps some people can see things other people can't see, Curdie," said his mother gravely. "I think I will tell you something I saw myself once—only perhaps you won't believe me either!"

"Oh, mother, mother!" cried Curdie, bursting into tears. "I don't deserve that, surely!"

"But what I am going to tell you is very strange," persisted his mother. "If having heard it you were to say I must have been dreaming, I don't know that I should have any right to be vexed with you, though I know at least that I was not asleep."

"Do tell me, mother. Perhaps it will help me to think better of the princess."

"That's why I am tempted to tell you," replied his mother. "But first, I may as well mention that, according to old whispers, there is something more than common about the king's family. There were strange stories told concerning them—all good stories—but strange, very strange. What they were I cannot tell, for I only remember the faces of my grandmother and my mother as they talked together about them. There was wonder in their eyes, and they whispered, and never spoke aloud.

"But what I saw myself was this: your father was going to work in the mine one night, and I had been down with his supper. It was soon after we were married, and not very long before you were born. He came with me to the mouth of the mine, and left me to go home alone; for I knew the way almost as well as the floor of our own cottage. It was pretty dark, but I got along perfectly well, never thinking of being afraid, until I reached a spot you know well enough, Curdie, where the path has to make a sharp turn out of the way of a great rock on the left-hand side. When I got there, I was suddenly surrounded by about half a dozen of the cobs, the first I had ever seen, although I had heard tell of them often enough. One of them blocked up the path, and they all began tormenting and teasing me in a way it makes me shudder to think of even now."

"If I had only been with you!" cried father and son in a breath.

The mother gave a funny little smile, and went on.

"They had some of their horrible creatures with them, too, and I must confess I was dreadfully frightened. They had torn my clothes very much, and I was afraid they were going to tear me to pieces, when suddenly a great white soft light shone upon me.

"I looked up. A broad ray, like a shining road, came down from a large globe of silvery light, not very high up, indeed not quite so high as the horizon, so it could not have been a new star or another moon or anything of that sort. The cobs stopped persecuting me, and looked dazed, and I thought they were going to run away, but presently they began again. The same moment, however, down the path from the globe of light came a bird, shining like silver in the sun. It gave a few rapid flaps first, and then, with its wings straight out, shot sliding down the slope of the light. It looked to me just like a white pigeon. But whatever it was, when the cobs caught sight of it coming straight down upon them, they took to their heels and scampered away across the mountain, leaving me safe, only much frightened. As soon as it had sent them off, the bird went gliding again up the light, and the moment it reached the globe the light disappeared, just as if a shutter had been closed over a window, and I saw it no more. But I had no more trouble with the cobs that night or ever after."

"How strange!" exclaimed Curdie.

"Yes, it was strange; but I can't help believing it, whether you do or not," said his mother.

"You don't think I'm doubting my own mother?" cried Curdie.

"There are other people in the world quite as well worth believing as your own mother," said she. "I don't know that I'm so much the fitter to be believed that I happen to be your mother, Mr. Curdie. There are mothers far more likely to tell lies than the little girl I saw talking to the primroses a few weeks ago. She's a good girl, I am certain, and that's more than being a princess. Depend upon it, you will have to be sorry for behaving so to her, Curdie. You ought at least to have held your tongue."

"I am sorry now."

"You ought to go and tell her so, then."

"I don't see how I could manage that. They wouldn't let a miner boy have a word with her alone; and I couldn't tell her before that nurse of hers. She'd be asking ever so many questions, and I don't know how many the little princess would like me to answer. But I may have a chance before long. Meantime I must try to do something for her. I think, father, I have got on the track at last."

"Have you, indeed, my boy?" said Peter. "What have you found out?"

"It's difficult, you know, father, inside the mountain, especially in the dark, and not knowing what turns you have taken, to tell the lie of things outside."

"Impossible, my boy, without a chart, or at least a compass," returned his father.

"Well, I think I have nearly discovered in what direction the cobs are mining. If I am right, I know something else that I can put to it, and then one and one will make three."

"They very often do, Curdie. Now tell us what the two things are, my boy, and see whether we can guess at the same third as you."

"Just as we came to the channel by which we got out, I heard the miners at work somewhere near—I think down below us. Now since I began to watch them, they have mined a good half mile, in a straight line. So far as I am aware, they are working in no other part of the mountain. But I never could tell in what direction they were going. When we came out in the king's garden, however, I thought at once whether it was possible they were working towards the king's house. What I want to do tonight is to make sure whether they are or not. I will take a light with me—"

"Oh, Curdie," cried his mother, "then they will see you."

"I'm no more afraid of them now than I was before," rejoined Curdie, "now that I've got this precious shoe. They can't make another in a hurry, and one bare foot will do for my purpose. Woman as she may be, I won't spare her next time. But I shall be careful with my light, for I don't want them to see me. I won't stick it on my hat."

"Go on, then, and tell us what you mean to do."

"I mean to take a bit of paper with me and a pencil, and go in at the mouth of the stream by which we came out. I shall mark on the paper as near as I can the angle of every turning I take until I find the cobs at work, and so get a good idea in what direction they are going. If it should prove to be nearly parallel with the stream, I shall know it is towards the king's house they are working.

"I told you that when I came upon the royal family in the cave, they were talking of their prince—Harelip, they called him—marrying a sun woman (that means one of us), one with toes to her feet. Now in the speech one of them made that night at their great gathering, he said that peace would be secured for a generation at least by the pledge the prince would hold for the good behavior of *her* relatives. That's what he said, and he must have meant the sun woman the prince was to marry. I am quite sure the king is much too proud to wish his son to marry any but a princess, and much too knowing to fancy that his having a peasant woman for a wife would be of any great advantage to them."

"I see what you are driving at now," said his mother.

"But," said his father, "our king would dig the mountain to the plain before he would have his princess the wife of a cob, if he were ten times a prince."

"I fancy," said Curdie, "if the cobs got her, they would tell the king they would kill her except he consented to the marriage."

"They might say so," said his father, "but they wouldn't kill her; they would keep her alive for the sake of the hold it gave them over our king. Whatever he did to them, they would threaten to do the same to the princess."

"And they are bad enough to torment her just for their own amusement, I know that," said his mother.

"It's too horrible to think of," said Curdie. "But they shan't have her—at least if I can help it. So, mother dear, will you get me a bit of paper and a pencil and a lump of pease pudding, and I will set out at once. I saw a place where I can climb over the wall of the garden quite easily."

"You must mind and keep out of the way of the men on the watch," said his mother.

"That I will. I don't want them to know anything about it. They would spoil it all. The cobs would only try some other plan."

His mother got him what he had asked for, and Curdie set out. Close beside the door by which the princess left the garden for the mountain stood a great rock, and by climbing it Curdie got over the wall. He tied his string to a stone just inside the channel of the stream, and took his pickax with him.

After exploring and measuring for some time, he was satisfied that the goblins were mining in the direction of the palace—on so low a level that their intention must, he thought, be to burrow under the walls of the king's house, and rise up inside it, in order to lay hands on the little princess and carry her off for a wife to their horrid Harelip.

14   Curdie Comes to Grief

When the princess awoke from the sweetest of sleeps, she found her nurse bending over her, the housekeeper looking over the nurse's shoulder, and the laundry maid looking over the housekeeper's. The room was full of women servants; and the gentlemen-at-arms, with a long column of servants behind them, were peeping, or trying to peep in at the door of the nursery.

"Are those horrid creatures gone?" asked the princess, remembering first what had terrified her in the morning.

"You naughty, naughty little princess!" cried Lootie.

Her face was very pale, with red streaks in it, and she looked as if she were going to shake her. But Irene said nothing, only waited to hear what should come next.

"How could you get under the clothes like that, and make us all fancy you were lost! And keep it up all day, too! You are the most obstinate child! It's anything but fun to us, I can tell you!"

It was the only way the nurse could account for her disappearance.

"I didn't do that, Lootie," said Irene, very quietly.

"Don't tell stories!" cried her nurse quite rudely.

"I shall tell you nothing at all," said Irene.

"That's just as bad."

"Just as bad to say nothing at all as to tell stories?" exclaimed the princess. "I will ask my papa about that. He won't say so. And I don't think he will like you to say so."

"Tell me directly what you mean by it!" screamed the nurse, half wild with anger at the princess and fright at the possible consequences to herself.

"When I tell you the truth, Lootie," said the princess, who somehow did not feel at all angry, "you say to me, 'Don't tell stories.' It seems I must tell stories before you will believe me."

"You are the most provoking child!" cried her nurse. "You deserve to be punished for your wicked behavior."

"Please, Mrs. Housekeeper," said the princess, "will you take me to your room, and keep me till my king-papa comes? I will ask him to come as soon as he can."

Everyone stared at these words. Up to this moment they had all regarded Irene as little more than a baby.

But the housekeeper was afraid of the nurse, and sought to patch matters up, saying, "I am sure, princess, nursie did not mean to be rude to you."

"I do not think my papa would wish me to have a nurse who spoke to me as Lootie does. If she thinks I tell lies, she had better either say so to my papa, or go away. Sir Walter, will you take charge of me?"

"With the greatest of pleasure, princess," answered the captain of the gentlemen-at-arms, walking with his great stride into the room. The crowd of servants made way for him, and he bowed low before the little princess's bed. "I shall send my servant at once, on the fastest horse in the stable, to tell your king-papa that Your Royal Highness desires his presence. When you have chosen one of these underservants to wait upon you, I shall order the room to be cleared."

"Thank you very much, Sir Walter," said the princess, and her eye glanced towards a rosy-cheeked girl who had lately come to the house as a scullery maid.

But when Lootie saw the eyes of her dear princess going in search of another instead of her, she fell upon her knees by the bedside, and burst into a great cry of distress.

"I think, Sir Walter," said the princess finally, "that I will keep Lootie. But I put myself under your care. You need not trouble my king-papa until I speak to you again. Will you all please to go away? I am quite safe and well, and I did not hide myself for the sake either of amusing myself or of troubling my people. Lootie, will you please to dress me?"

Everything was for some time quiet above ground. The king was still away in a distant part of his dominions. The men-at-arms kept watching about the house. Curdie kept watching in the mountain, and the goblins kept burrowing deeper into the earth. As long as they went deeper there was, Curdie judged, no immediate danger.

To Irene the summer was as full of pleasure as ever, and for a long time, although she often thought of her grandmother during the day, and often dreamed about her at night, she did not see her. The animals and the flowers were as much her delight as ever, and she made as much friendship with the miners' children she met on the mountain as Lootie would permit; but Lootie had very foolish notions concerning the dignity of a princess. At the same time she was considerably altered for the better in her behavior to the princess. She could not help seeing that she was no longer a mere child, but wiser than her age would account for.

All this time Curdie had to be sorry, without a chance of confessing, that he had behaved so unkindly to the princess. This perhaps made him the more diligent in his endeavors to serve her. Here I should like to remark, for the sake of princes and princesses in general, that it is a low and contemptible thing to refuse to confess a fault. If a true princess has done wrong, she is always uneasy until she has had an opportunity of throwing the wrongness away from her by saying: "I did it, and I wish I had not, and I am sorry for having done it." So you see there is some ground for supposing that Curdie was not a miner only, but a prince as well. Many such instances have been known in the world's history.

At length, Curdie began to see signs of a change in the proceedings of the goblin excavators. They were going no deeper, but had commenced running on a level. He watched them, therefore, more closely than ever. All at once, one night, coming to a slope of very hard rock, they began to ascend along the inclined plane of its surface at a pretty steep angle.

The next night Curdie did not go to the mine at all. Leaving his pickax and string at home, and taking only his usual lumps of bread and pease pudding, he went down the mountain to the king's house. He climbed over the wall, and remained in the garden the whole night, creeping on hands and knees from one spot to the other, and lying at full length with his ear to the ground, listening. But he heard nothing except the tread of the men-at-arms as they marched about. For several following nights he continued to haunt the garden and listen, but with no success.

At length, early one evening, whether it was that he had gotten careless of his own safety, or that the growing moon had become strong enough to expose

103

him, his watching came to a sudden end. He was creeping from behind the rock where the stream ran out, for he had been listening all round it in the hope it might convey to his ear some indication of the whereabouts of the goblin miners. Just as he came into the moonlight on the lawn, a whiz in his ear and a blow upon his leg startled him.

He instantly squatted in the hope of eluding further notice. But when he heard the sound of running feet, he jumped up to take the chance of escape by flight. He fell, however, with a keen stab of pain, for the bolt of a crossbow had wounded his leg, and the blood was now streaming from it. He was instantly laid hold of by two or three of the men-at-arms. It was useless to struggle, and he submitted in silence.

"It's a boy!" cried several of them together, in a tone of amazement. "I thought it was one of those demons."

"What are you about here?"

"Going to have a little rough usage, apparently," said Curdie, laughing, as the men shook him.

"Impertinence will do you no good. You have no business here in the king's grounds. If you don't give a true account of yourself, you shall fare as a thief."

"Why, what else could he be?" said one.

"He might have been after a lost lamb, you know," suggested another.

"I see no good in trying to excuse him. He has no business here, anyhow."

"Let me go away, then, if you please," said Curdie.

"But we don't please, not except you give a good account of yourself."

"I don't feel quite sure whether I can trust you," said Curdie.

"We are the king's own men-at-arms," said the captain courteously, for he was taken with Curdie's appearance and courage.

"Well, I will tell you all about it—if you will promise to listen to me and not do anything rash."

"I call that cool!" said one of the party, laughing. "He will tell us what mischief he was about, if we promise to do as pleases him."

"I was about no mischief," said Curdie.

But ere he could say more he turned faint, and fell senseless on the grass. Then they discovered that the bolt they had shot, taking him for one of the goblin creatures, had wounded him.

They carried him into the house and laid him down in the hall. The report spread that they had caught a robber, and the servants crowded in to see the villain. Amongst the rest came the nurse. The moment she saw him she exclaimed with indignation: "I declare it's the same young rascal of a miner

104

that was rude to me and the princess on the mountain. He actually wanted to kiss the princess. And *he* was prowling about—was he? Just like his impudence!"

When he heard this, the captain resolved to keep Curdie a prisoner until they could search into the affair. So, after they had brought him round a little, and attended to his wound, which was rather a bad one, they laid him, still exhausted from the loss of blood, upon a mattress in a disused room, and locked the door, and left him.

He passed a troubled night, and in the morning they found him talking wildly. In the evening he came to himself, but felt very weak, and his leg was exceedingly painful. Wondering where he was, and seeing one of the men-at-arms in the room, he began to question him, and soon recalled the events of the preceding night. As he was himself unable to watch anymore, he told the soldier all he knew about the goblins, and begged him to tell his companions, and stir them up to watch with tenfold vigilance. But whether it was that he did not talk quite coherently or that the whole thing appeared incredible, the man concluded that Curdie was only raving still, and tried to coax him into holding his tongue. This, of course, annoyed Curdie dreadfully, and the consequence was that his fever returned. By the time the captain was called at Curdie's persistent entreaties, there could be no doubt that he was raving. They did for him what they could, and promised everything he wanted, but with no intention of fulfillment. At last he went to sleep. When at length his sleep grew profound and peaceful, they left him, locked the door again, and withdrew, intending to revisit him early in the morning.

That same night several of the servants were having a chat together before going to bed. "What can that noise be?" said one of the housemaids, who had been listening for a moment or two.

"I've heard it the last two nights," said the cook. "I should have taken it for rats, but my cat keeps them far enough."

"I've heard, though," said the scullery maid, "that rats move about in great companies sometimes. There may be an army of them invading us. I've heard the noises yesterday and today, too."

"It seems to me," said the nurse, "that the noises are much too loud for rats. I have heard them all day, and my princess has asked me several times what they could be. Sometimes they sound like distant thunder, and sometimes like the noises you hear in the mountain from those horrid miners underneath. They are always boring and blasting and breaking, you know."

As she spoke, there came a great, rolling rumble beneath them, and the house quivered. They all started up in affright, and rushing to the hall found the gentlemen-at-arms in consternation also. They had sent to wake their captain, who said that it must have been an earthquake, an occurrence which, although very rare in that country, had taken place almost within the century. He then went to bed again, strange to say, and fell fast asleep without once thinking of Curdie, or associating the noises they had heard with what the boy had told them.

He had not believed Curdie. If he had, he would at once have taken precautions. The fact was that the goblins had arrived at a huge block, which lay under the cellars of the house, within the line of the foundations. It was so round that when they succeeded in dislodging it, the block rolled thundering down the underground slope with a bounding, jarring roll, which shook the foundations of the house.

The goblins were themselves dismayed at the noise, for they knew, by careful spying and measuring, that they must now be very near—if not under—the king's house, and they feared giving an alarm. They, therefore, remained quiet for a while, then began to work again quietly until they came out in the king's wine cellar.

No sooner did they find where they were, than they scurried back again, like rats into their holes, and running at full speed to the goblin palace, announced their success to the king with shouts of triumph. In a moment he and the queen, who stumped along in one shoe of stone and one of animal skin, and the whole goblin people were on their way in hot haste to the king's house, each eager to share in the glory of carrying off Princess Irene.

15 Goblins in the King's House

When Curdie fell asleep he began at once to dream. He thought he was ascending the mountainside from the mouth of the mine, whistling and singing, "Ring, dod, bang!" when he came upon a woman and child who had lost their way. From that point he went on dreaming everything that had happened to him since he had met the princess and Lootie—everything, indeed, until he was wounded, captured, and imprisoned by the men-at-arms. Now he thought he was lying wide awake where they had laid him, when suddenly he heard a great thundering sound.

"The cobs are coming!" he said. "They didn't believe a word I told them! The cobs'll be carrying off the princess from under their stupid noses! But they shan't! That they shan't!"

He jumped up, as he thought, and began to dress, but to his dismay, found that he was still lying in bed. For in fact he was not awake, only dreaming that he was. At length in an agony of despair, fancying he heard the goblins all over the house, he gave a great cry. Then there came, as he thought, a hand upon the lock of his door. It opened, and, looking up, he saw a lady with white hair, carrying a silver box in her hand. She came to his bed, stroked his head and face with cool, soft hands, took the dressing from his leg, rubbed it with something that smelled like roses, and then waved her hands over him three times. At the last wave of her hands everything vanished. He felt himself sinking into the profoundest slumber, and remembered nothing more until he awoke in earnest.

The setting moon was throwing a feeble light through the casement, and the house was full of uproar. There was heavy stamping, a clashing and clanging of weapons, the voices of men and the cries of women, mixed with a hideous bellowing. Curdie sprang from his bed, hurried on some of his clothes, not forgetting his shoes, which were armed with nails. Then spying an old hunting knife, or short sword, hanging on the wall, he caught it, and rushed down the stairs, guided by the sounds of strife, which grew louder and louder.

When he reached the ground floor, he found the whole place swarming. All the goblins of the mountain seemed gathered there. He rushed amongst them, shouting:

> "One, two,
> Hit and hew!
> Three, Four,
> Blast and bore!"

With every rhyme he came down a great stamp upon a goblin foot, cutting at the same time at their faces—executing, indeed, a sword dance of the wildest description. The goblins scattered in every direction: into closets, up stairs, into chimneys, up on rafters, and down to the cellars. Curdie went on stamping and slashing and singing, but saw nothing of the people of the house until he came to the great hall. The moment he entered, a great goblin shout arose. The last of the men-at-arms, the captain himself, was on the floor, buried beneath a wallowing crowd of goblins. The cobs would have torn them all to pieces, but the king had given orders to carry them away alive, and over each of the twelve was standing a knot of goblins, while as many as could find room were sitting upon the men's prostrate bodies.

Curdie burst in dancing and gyrating and stamping and singing like a small whirlwind.

> "Where 'tis all a hole, sir,
> Never can be holes:
> Why should their shoes have soles, sir,
> When they've got no souls?
>
> "But she upon her foot, sir,
> Has a granite shoe:
> The strongest leather boot, sir,
> Six toes would soon push through."

The queen gave a howl of rage and dismay; and before she recovered her presence of mind, Curdie, beginning with the group nearest him, had eleven of the knights on their legs again.

"Stamp on their feet!" he cried as each man rose. In a few minutes the hall was nearly empty, the goblins running from it as fast as they could—howling and shrieking and limping—and cowering every now and then as they ran to cuddle their wounded feet in their hard hands, or to protect them from the frightful *stamp stamp* of the armed men.

Now Curdie approached the group which, trusting in the queen and her one shoe, kept guard over the prostrate captain. The king sat on the captain's head, but the queen stood in front, like an infuriated cat, with her perpendicular eyes gleaming green and her hair standing half up from her horrid head. Her heart was quaking, however, and she kept moving about the foot in the animal skin shoe with nervous apprehension.

When Curdie was within a few paces, she rushed at him, made one tremendous stamp at his opposing foot, which happily he withdrew in time, and caught him round the waist to dash him on the marble floor. But just as she caught him, he came down with all the weight of his iron-shod shoe upon her skin-shod foot. With a hideous howl she dropped him, squatted on the floor, and took her foot in both her hands. Meanwhile the rest rushed on the king and the bodyguards, sent them flying, and lifted the prostrate captain, who was all but pressed to death. It was some moments before he recovered.

"Where's the princess?" cried Curdie again and again.

No one knew, and off they all rushed in search of her. Through every room in the house they went, but nowhere was she to be found. Neither was one of the servants to be seen. But Curdie, who had kept to the lower part of the house, which was now quiet enough, began to hear a confused sound as of a distant hubbub, and set out to find where it came from. The noise grew as his sharp ears guided him to a stair and so to the wine cellar. It was full of goblins, whom the butler was supplying with wine as fast as he could pour it.

While the queen and her party had encountered the men-at-arms, Harelip with another company had gone off to search the house. They captured everyone they met. When they could find no more, they hurried away to carry them safe to the caverns below. But when the butler, who was amongst them, found that their path lay through the wine cellar, he persuaded them to taste the wine. As he had hoped, they no sooner tasted it than they wanted more. The routed goblins joined them, and when Curdie entered they held vessels of every description, from saucepan to silver cup, and were all pressing around the butler, who sat at the tap of a huge cask, filling and filling.

Curdie cast one glance around the place before commencing his attack, and saw in the farthest corner a terrified group of the servants unwatched, but cowering without any courage to attempt their escape. Amongst them was the terror-stricken face of Lootie. Nowhere could he see the princess. Seized with the horrible conviction that Harelip had already carried her off, he rushed amongst them, unable for wrath to sing anymore, but stamping and cutting with greater fury than ever.

"Stamp on their feet. Stamp on their feet!" he shouted. In a moment the goblins were disappearing through the hole in the floor like rats and mice.

Presently, the goblins were reinforced from above by the goblin king and his party, with the queen at their head. Finding Curdie busy amongst her unfortunate subjects, she rushed at him once more with the rage of despair, and this time gave him a bad bruise on the foot. Then a regular stamping fight got up between them, Curdie, with the point of his hunting knife, keeping her from clasping her mighty arms about him, as he watched his opportunity of getting a good stamp at her skin-shod foot. But the queen was more wary as well as more agile than before.

The rest of the goblins, finding their enemy thus matched for the moment, paused in their headlong hurry, and turned to the shivering group of women in the corner. As if determined to emulate his father and have a sun woman of some sort to share his future throne, Harelip rushed at them, caught up Lootie, and sped with her to the hole. She gave a great shriek, and Curdie saw the plight she was in. Gathering all his strength, he gave the queen a sudden cut across the face with his weapon, came down with all his weight on the proper foot, and sprung to Lootie's rescue. The prince had two defenseless feet, and on both of them Curdie stamped just as he reached the hole. Harelip dropped his burden and rolled shrieking into the earth. Curdie made one stab at him as he disappeared, caught hold of the senseless Lootie, and dragged her back to the corner, where he mounted guard over her and prepared once more to encounter the queen.

Her eyes flashing green lightning, the queen came on with her mouth open and her teeth grinning like a tiger's, followed by the king and her bodyguard of the thickest goblins. But at the same moment, in rushed the captain and his men, and ran at them stamping furiously. The goblins dared not encounter such an onset. Away they scurried, the queen foremost. Of course, the right thing would have been to take the king and queen prisoners, and hold them hostages for the princess, but they were so anxious to find her that no one

111

thought of detaining them until it was too late.

Having thus rescued the servants, they searched the house once more. None of them could give the least information concerning the princess. Lootie was almost silly with terror, and although scarcely able to walk, would not leave Curdie's side. Again he allowed the others to search the rest of the house—where, except a dismayed goblin lurking here and there, they found no one—while he requested Lootie to take him to the princess's room. She was as submissive and obedient as if he had been the king.

He found the bedclothes tossed about, and most of them on the floor, while the princess's garments were scattered all over the room, which was in the greatest confusion. It was only too evident that the goblins had been there. Curdie had no longer any doubt that she had been carried off at the very first of the inroad. With a pang of despair he saw how wrong they had been in not securing the king and queen and prince. He determined to find and rescue the princess as she had found and rescued him, or meet the worst fate to which the goblins could doom him.

Just as this resolve dawned upon his mind and he was turning away for the cellar to follow the goblins into their hole, something touched his hand. It was the slightest touch, and when he looked he could see nothing. Feeling and peering about in the gray of the dawn, his fingers came upon a tight thread.

He looked again, but still could see nothing. It flashed upon him that this must be the princess's thread. Without saying a word, for he knew no one would believe him any more than he had believed the princess, he followed the thread with his finger, contrived to give Lootie the slip, and was soon out of the house and on the mountainside—surprised that, if the thread were indeed the grandmother's messenger, it should have led the princess, as he supposed it must, into the mountain, where she would be certain to meet the goblins rushing back enraged from their defeat. But he hurried on in the hope of overtaking her before they did.

When he arrived at the place where the path turned off for the mine, he found that the thread did not turn with it, but went straight up the mountain. Could it be that the thread was leading him home to his mother's cottage? Could the princess be there? He bounded up the mountain, and before the sun was up the thread had brought him indeed to his mother's door. There it vanished from his fingers, and he could not find it, search as he might.

The door was unlatched, and he entered. There sat his mother by the fire, and in her arms lay the princess fast asleep.

"Hush, Curdie!" said his mother. "Do not wake her. I'm so glad you've

114

come! I thought the cobs must have got you again!"

With a heart full of delight, Curdie sat down on a stool opposite his mother's chair, and gazed at the princess, who slept as peacefully as if she had been in her own bed. All at once she opened her eyes and fixed them on him.

"Oh, Curdie! you've come!" she said quietly. "I thought you would!"

Curdie rose and stood before her with downcast eyes. "Irene," he said, "I am very sorry I did not believe you."

"Oh, never mind, Curdie!" answered the princess. "You couldn't, you know. You do believe me now, don't you?"

"I can't help it now. I ought to have helped it before."

"Why can't you help it now?"

"Because, just as I was going into the mountain to look for you, I got hold of your thread, and it brought me here."

"Then you've come from my house, have you? I didn't know you were there."

"I've been there two or three days, I believe."

"And I never knew it! Then perhaps you can tell me why my grandmother has brought me here. I can't think. Something woke me—I didn't know what, but I was frightened, and I felt for the thread, and there it was! I was more frightened still when it brought me out on the mountain, for I thought it was going to take me into it again, and I like the outside of it best. But it brought me here instead. Oh, Curdie! your mother has been so kind to me—just like my own grandmother!"

"Then you didn't see the cobs?" asked Curdie.

"No, I haven't been into the mountain, I told you, Curdie."

"But the cobs have been into your house—all over it—and into your bedroom, making such a row! They wanted to carry you off into the mountain with them, for a wife to their Prince Harelip."

"Oh, how dreadful!" cried the princess, shuddering.

"But you needn't be afraid, you know. Your grandmother takes care of you."

"Ah! you do believe in my grandmother, then? I'm so glad! She made me think you would someday."

All at once Curdie remembered his dream, and was silent, thinking.

"But how did you come to be in my house, and me not know it?" asked the princess.

Then Curdie had to explain everything: how he had watched for her sake, how he had been wounded and shut up by the soldiers, and how the beautiful old lady had come to him, and all that followed.

"Poor Curdie! To lie there hurt and ill, and me never to know it!" exclaimed the princess, stroking his rough hand. "I would have come and nursed you, if they had told me."

"I didn't see you were lame," said his mother.

"Am I, mother? Oh—yes—I suppose I ought to be. I declare I've never thought of it since I got up to go down amongst the cobs!"

"Let me see the wound," said his mother.

He pulled down his stocking. Except for a great scar, his leg was perfectly sound!

Curdie and his mother gazed in each other's eyes, full of wonder, but Irene called out, "I thought so, Curdie! I was sure it wasn't a dream. I was sure my grandmother had been to see you. Don't you smell the roses? It was my grandmother who healed your leg, and sent you to help me and my people."

"So it seems," said the mother. "But we are forgetting how frightened your people must be. You must take the princess home at once, Curdie—or at least go and tell them where she is."

"Yes, mother. Only I'm dreadfully hungry. Do let me have some breakfast first. They ought to have listened to me: then they wouldn't have been taken by surprise."

"That is true, Curdie; but it is not for you to blame them much for not believing. You remember?"

"Yes, mother, I do. Only I must really have something to eat."

"Yes, you shall, my boy—as fast as I can get it," said his mother, rising and setting the princess on her chair.

But before his breakfast was ready, Curdie jumped up so suddenly as to startle both his companions.

"Mother, mother!" he cried. "I was forgetting. You must take the princess home yourself. I must go and wake my father."

Without a word of explanation, he rushed to the place where his father was sleeping. Having thoroughly roused him with what he told him, he darted out of the cottage.

He had all at once remembered the resolution of the goblins to carry out their second plan upon the failure of the first. No doubt they were already busy, and the mine was therefore in the greatest danger of being flooded and rendered useless—not to speak of the danger to the lives of the miners.

When he reached the mouth of the mine and had roused all the miners within reach, he found a good many more just entering. They all hurried to the gang by which Curdie had found a way into the goblin country. There his

116

father had already collected a great many blocks of stone, with cement, ready for building up the weak place known to the goblins. Although there was not room for more than two to be building at once, the miners managed, by setting all the rest to work in preparing the cement and passing the stones, to finish in the course of the day a huge buttress filling the whole gang, and supported everywhere by the live rock. Before the hour when they usually dropped work, they were satisfied the mine was secure from flooding.

They had heard goblin hammers and pickaxes busy all the time, and at length fancied they heard sounds of water. But that was otherwise accounted for when they left the mine, for they stepped out into a tremendous storm, which was raging all over the mountain. The thunder was bellowing, and the lightning lancing out of a huge black cloud, which lay above it and hung down its edges of thick mist over its sides. The lightning was breaking out of the mountain, too, and flashing up into the cloud.

The wind was blowing as if it would blow him off the mountain, but, anxious about his mother and the princess, Curdie darted through the thick of the tempest. The moment his hand fell on the latch, through all the uproar of winds and waters came the joyous cry of the princess: "There's Curdie! Curdie! Curdie!"

She sat wrapped in blankets on the bed, his mother trying for the hundredth time to light the fire, which had been drowned by the rain that came down the chimney. The clay floor was one mass of mud, and the whole place looked wretched. But the faces of the mother and the princess shone as if their troubles only made them the merrier. Curdie burst out laughing at the sight of them.

"I never had such fun!" said the princess, her eyes twinkling. "How nice it must be to live in a cottage on the mountain!"

By the time Curdie's father returned the storm was nearly over, but the streams were so fierce and swollen that it was not only out of the question for the princess to go down the mountain, but most dangerous for Peter or even Curdie to make the attempt in the gathering darkness.

"They will be dreadfully frightened about you," said Peter to the princess, "but we cannot help it. We must wait till the morning."

With Curdie's help, the fire was lighted at last, and the mother set about making their supper. After supper they all told the princess stories till she grew sleepy. Then Curdie's mother laid her in Curdie's bed, which was in a tiny little garret room. As soon as she was in bed, through a little window low down in the roof, she caught sight of her grandmother's lamp shining far away. She gazed at the beautiful silver globe until she fell asleep.

16 The Underground Waters

The next morning the sun rose so bright that Irene said the rain had washed his face and let the light out clean. The torrents were still roaring down the side of the mountain, but they were so much smaller as not to be dangerous in the daylight. After an early breakfast, Peter went to his work and Curdie and his mother set out to take the princess home. They had difficulty in getting her across the streams; Curdie had again and again to carry her. At last they got safe on the broader part of the road, and walked gently down towards the king's house. What should they see as they turned the last corner but the last of the king's troop riding through the gate!

"Oh, Curdie!" cried Irene, clapping her hands. "My king-papa is come."

The moment Curdie heard that, he caught her up in his arms, and set off at full speed, crying, "Come on, mother dear! The king may break his heart before he knows that she is safe."

Irene clung around his neck and he ran with her like a deer. When he entered the gate into the court, the king sat on his horse, with all the people of the house about him, weeping and hanging their heads. The king was not weeping, but his face was white as a dead man's, and he looked as if the life had gone out of him. The men-at-arms he had brought with him sat with horror-stricken faces, but eyes flashing with rage, waiting only for the word of the king to do something—they did not know what.

The day before, the men-at-arms belonging to the house, as soon as they were satisfied the princess had been carried away, rushed after the goblins into the hole, but found that the goblins had already so skillfully blockaded the narrowest part, not many feet below the cellar, that without miners and their tools they could do nothing. Not one of them knew where the mouth of the mine lay, and some of those who had set out to find it had been overtaken by the storm and had not even yet returned. Poor Sir Walter was especially filled with shame, and almost hoped the king would order his head to be cut off, for to think of that sweet little face down amongst the goblins was unendurable.

When Curdie ran in at the gate with the princess in his arms, they were all so absorbed in their own misery and awed by the king's presence and grief, that no one observed his arrival. He went straight up to the king, where he sat on his horse.

"Papa! papa!" the princess cried, stretching out her arms to him. "Here I am!"

The king started. The color rushed to his face. He gave an inarticulate cry. Curdie held up the princess, and the king bent down and took her from his arms. As he clasped her to his bosom, the big tears went dropping down his cheeks and his beard. Such a shout arose from all the bystanders that the startled horses pranced and capered, and the armor rang and clattered, and the rocks of the mountain echoed back the noise.

The princess greeted them all as she nestled in her father's bosom, and the king did not set her down until she had told them all the story. But she had more to tell about Curdie than about herself, and what she did tell about herself none of them could understand except the king and Curdie, who stood by the king's knee stroking the neck of the great white horse. As she told what Curdie had done, Sir Walter and others added to what she told, even Lootie joining in the praises of his courage and energy.

Curdie held his peace, looking quietly up in the king's face. And his mother stood on the outskirts of the crowd listening with delight, for her son's deeds were pleasant in her ears.

"And now, king-papa," the princess went on, "I must tell you another thing. One night long ago Curdie drove the goblins away and brought Lootie and me safe from the mountain. I promised him a kiss when we got home, but Lootie wouldn't let me give it to him. I don't want you to scold Lootie, but I want you to tell her that a princess must do as she promises."

"Indeed she must, my child—except it be wrong," said the king. "There, give Curdie a kiss."

The princess reached down, threw her arms round Curdie's neck, and kissed him on the mouth, saying, "There, Curdie! There's the kiss I promised you!"

Then they all went into the house, and the cook rushed to the kitchen and the servants to their work. Lootie dressed Irene in her shiniest clothes, and the king put off his armor and put on purple and gold. A messenger was sent to fetch Peter and all the miners, and there was a great and grand feast, which continued long after the princess was put to bed.

The king's harper, who always formed a part of his escort, was chanting a ballad about the princess and the goblins and the prowess of Curdie, when all at once he ceased, his eyes on one of the doors of the hall. Thereupon the eyes of the king and his guests turned there also. Through the open doorway came the Princess Irene. She went straight up to her father, with her right hand stretched out a little sideways and her forefinger, as her father and Curdie understood, feeling its way along the invisible thread. The king took her on his knee, and she said in his ear, "King-papa, do you hear that noise?"

"I hear nothing," said the king.

"Listen," she said, holding up her forefinger.

The king listened, and each man, seeing that the king listened, listened also.

"I do hear a noise," said the king at length. "A noise as of distant thunder. It is coming nearer and nearer. What can it be?"

"I think it must be another storm coming over the mountain," said Sir Walter.

Then Curdie, who at the first word of the king had slipped from his seat and laid his ear to the ground, rose up quickly, and approaching the king said, speaking very fast: "Please, Your Majesty, I think I know what it is. I have no time to explain, for that might make it too late for some of us. Will Your Majesty give orders that everybody leave the house as quickly as possible and get up the mountain?"

The king, who was the wisest man in the land, knew well there was a time when things must be done and questions left till afterwards. He had faith in Curdie, and rose instantly, with Irene in his arms.

"Every man and woman follow me at once," he said, and strode out into the darkness.

Before he had reached the gate, the noise had grown to a great thundering roar, and the ground trembled beneath their feet. As the last of them crossed

the court, a huge rush of turbid water came out after them from the great hall door and almost swept them away. But they got safely out of the gate and up the mountain, while the torrent went roaring down the road into the valley beneath.

Curdie had left the king and the princess to look after his mother, whom he and his father had caught up and carried to safety.

When the king had gotten out of the way of the water, a little up the mountain, he stood with the princess in his arms, looking back with amazement on the torrent, which glimmered fierce and foamy through the night. There Curdie rejoined them.

"Now, Curdie," said the king, "what does this mean? Is this what you expected?"

"It is, Your Majesty," said Curdie, and proceeded to tell him about the second scheme of the goblins to flood the mine and drown the miners. Then he explained what the miners had done to prevent it.

The goblins had, meanwhile, let loose all the underground reservoirs and streams, expecting the water to run down into the mine, which was lower than their part of the mountain. But the readiest outlet the water could find had turned out to be the tunnel they had made to the king's house, the possibility of which had not occurred to the young miner until he had laid his ear to the floor of the hall.

What was to be done? The house appeared in danger of falling, and every moment the torrent was increasing.

"We must leave here at once," said the king. "But how to get at the horses!"

"Shall I see if we can manage that?" said Curdie.

"Do," said the king.

Curdie took the men-at-arms over the garden wall and to the stables. They found their horses in terror; the water was rising fast around them, and it was quite time they got out. But there was no way, except by riding them through the stream, which was now pouring from the lower windows as well as the door. Curdie got on the king's white charger and, leading the way, brought them all in safety to the higher ground.

"Look, look, Curdie!" cried Irene, the moment that he led the horse up to the king.

Curdie did look, and saw, high in the air, somewhere about the top of the king's house, a great globe of light, shining like the purest silver.

"Oh!" he cried in some consternation, "that is your grandmother's lamp! We *must* get her out. I will go and find her. The house may fall, you know."

122

"My grandmother is in no danger," said Irene, smiling.

"Here, Curdie, take the princess while I get on my horse," said the king.

Curdie took the princess again, and both turned their eyes to the globe of light. The same moment there shot from it a white bird, which, descending with outstretched wings, made one circle round the king and Curdie and the princess, and then glided up again. The light and the pigeon vanished together.

"Now, Curdie," said the princess, as he lifted her back to her father's arms, "you see my grandmother knows all about it, and isn't frightened. I believe she could walk through that water and it wouldn't wet her a bit."

"But, my child," said the king, "you will be cold if you haven't something more on. Run, Curdie, my boy, and fetch anything you can lay your hands on to keep the princess warm. We have a long ride before us."

Curdie was gone in a moment, and soon returned with a great, rich fur and the news that dead goblins were tossing about in the current through the house. They had been caught in their own snare. Instead of the mine, they had flooded their own country and were now swept up drowned. Irene shuddered, but the king held her close to his bosom.

Then he turned to Sir Walter, and said, "Bring Curdie's father and mother here."

"I wish," said the king, when they stood before him, "to take your son with me. He shall enter my bodyguard at once, and wait further promotion."

Peter and his wife, overcome, only murmured almost inaudible thanks. But Curdie spoke aloud.

"Please, Your Majesty," he said, "I cannot leave my father and mother."

"That's right, Curdie!" cried the princess. "I wouldn't if I were you."

The king looked at the princess and then at Curdie with a glow of satisfaction on his countenance.

"I, too, think you are right, Curdie," he said, "and I will not ask you again. But I shall have a chance of doing something for you sometime."

"Your Majesty has already allowed me to serve you," said Curdie.

"But, Curdie," said his mother, "why shouldn't you go with the king? We can get on very well without you."

"But I can't get on very well without you. The king is very kind, but I could not be half the use to him that I am to you. Please, Your Majesty, if you wouldn't mind giving my mother a red petticoat! I should have gotten her one long ago, but for the goblins."

"As soon as we get home, Irene and I will search out the warmest one to be

123

found, and send it by one of the gentlemen."

"Yes, that we will, Curdie!" said the princess. "And next summer we'll come back and see you wear it, Curdie's mother. Shan't we, king-papa?"

"Yes, my love; I hope so." Turning to the miners, the king said, "Will you do the best you can for my servants tonight? I hope they will be able to return to the house tomorrow."

The miners with one voice promised their hospitality.

Then the king commanded his servants to mind whatever Curdie should say to them. After shaking hands with him and his father and mother, the king and the princess and all their company rode away down the side of the newly formed stream, which had already devoured half the road, into the starry night.

Curdie and his father and mother and all the rest went up the mountain. And the whole way a silvery light shone upon their path.